A Warrior's Will

Also by Justus Roux

My Master
Master's Ecstasy
Obey!
Sweet Rapture
Mistress Angelique
Wrath's Lust
Protector of My Heart
Keeper of My Soul
Heavenly Surrender
Breathless
Ayden's Awakening

Edited by Justus Roux
Erotic Tales
Erotic Fantasy: Tales of the Paranormal
Who's Your Daddy?

Justus Roux's website www.justusroux.com
Where erotica and love know no boundaries

ISBN 0-9754080-8-9

This book is dedicated to everyone that supported and encouraged me over the years

4

Chapter 1

Nina finished packing her workout clothes. Oh, God did she need her training today. It had been one of those days; hell it has been one of those months. It all started when she caught Jason cheating on her. Of course she kicked his ass right out of their apartment. She wasn't the forgive and forget kind of woman. Then her job, oh she really hated her job. Being a secretary for some old horny guy wasn't her idea of a dream job. If she didn't need the paycheck every week, she would have shown her boss some of her karate moves.

She bowed respectfully at her trainer then left the gym. It was already getting dark out as she headed for her car. She did her usual prayer as she turned the key, hoping that her piece of crap car would start. She laid her head on the steering wheel when the clicking sound she has grown to hate happened as she turned the key.

"God damn it," she muttered. She wasn't in the mood for the two-mile walk back to her apartment.

Slowly she climbed out of her car. She grabbed her purse and started the long walk back home. But before she left the parking lot a bright light blinded her. She tried to stand still as a rush of wind hit her.

"What the hell?" she exclaimed.

"Rai, here is a female."

Nina readied herself for whoever was coming. Judging by the guy's deep voice and heavy footsteps he was a big dude.

"I have the other female in the ship already. Let's hurry and grab this one," Rai said as he too closed in on Nina.

"I still don't understand why Niro will only allow us to take two females. There are so many beautiful females on this planet," Samson grumbled.

"Planet?" Nina gasped as she backed away from the men. She couldn't make out what they looked like yet. The bright light was still blinding her. She ran to the other side of the parking lot then quickly turned around. "Holy crap!" she exclaimed when she finally could make out her attackers. Two very large, barbarian-looking guys, and holy hell, they even wore loincloths and had swords strapped to their backs.

"Calm down female," Rai said as he slowly approached her. "I won't hurt you."

"What mental home did you two escape from?" Nina readied herself to fight.

"Mental home?"

"Come on Rai grab the female and let's go. The Rundal said they couldn't hold the orbit long. We have little time left."

Nina rushed at the large man and did her best roundhouse kick across his chest. This knocked him back. The other large male rushed at her. She evaded his grasp.

"This one has fire in her Rai." Samson chuckled.

"Yeah big boy, I got lots of fire in me and you are about to get burned." Nina came at him. She jumped up and front kicked Samson hard on his chest. This surprised him. But he quickly gathered himself and charged at her at the same time Rai did.

"Oh damn it," Nina cursed. There was no way she could take on them both and soon she found herself thrown over Rai's shoulder. "Put me down, asshole." She pounded on his back.

They walked into a bright light and she felt a strange pulling, almost a tickling sensation. The next moment she found herself inside what appeared to be a spaceship.

Rai put her down inside a room then left her there alone.

"There is no way…" she said as she looked around the room. "My cheese has finally slipped off its cracker." She rubbed her eyes then looked at the room again. "Either this is some sci-fi shit here, or I am completely crazy." She slowly sat down on what appears to be a bed. She ran her hands over the soft fur that covered the bed. Soon the fear started to seep in. Where in the hell was she? More importantly who were those men and what did they plan on doing with her? She lay down on the bed and wrapped the fur around her.

ဆဝဆဝဆဝ

"Rai, which female do you wish to play with," Samson said.

"I want the little one with fire in her soul. Sport should be very interesting with this one."

Samson chuckled and patted Rai on the back. Rai had won the Trials this year and was entitled to become protector for one of the new Earth females. Samson was chosen because Demos declined to travel to Earth. Demos won the Trials a year ago, but he wanted to stay on Malka to watch over Niro's mate Robin while she was with child.

Rai still didn't like the fact Niro wouldn't allow more than just two females taken or worse, that this was the only trip back to Earth since the first time. Niro wanted to make sure Robin would be able to have his child without any harm coming to her. Saa's mate Sabrina was pregnant too, but she was only a few months along.

Still, most warriors were happy Niro was now the leader of the Dascon clan. Niro's father, Hakan has grown very ill over the last year and he handed the burden of leadership over to Niro. No battle, no nothing, he just told the Clan this was how it was going to be. No warrior would dare challenge Niro and Hakan knew this. But Niro's concern over these Earth women's safety was frustrating to Rai and quite a few of the other males. They needed females and Earth was filled with so many beautiful ones.

Rai's cock grew harder the closer he got to the chamber that held his prize female. It had been so long since he had been with a female. The last time he was with a female was right after he won the Trials. He groaned as his lust filled his body. Demos was a fool to pass up having one of these Earth females. Oh, he was going to pin the female under him and ram his cock to the hilt into her sweet pussy, then he was going to ride her until she screamed his name out in pleasure.

Rai opened the door and saw Nina lying on the bed. He groaned loudly and rushed the bed.

Nina looked up and saw the large barbarian charging at her. She jumped quickly from the bed just before he grabbed her.

"You are mine and I want some sport." Rai quickly climbed out of the bed.

Nina could see the lust in his eyes and not to mention the very impressive bulge in his loincloth. "I don't think so buddy." She did a quick check of the room to see if there was anything she could use as a weapon.

"I won't hurt you, female." He slowly moved toward her. One way or another, his cock was going to be buried deeply into her.

"My name is Nina, not female and if you step one more foot closer to me, I swear I am going to hurt you."

"Hah, you are but a small female, do you really believe you can hurt me?"

"If you come any closer I guess we are going to find out." Nina backed up a little more. This big ox wasn't planning on just going away, so she really had no choice but to hurt him.

"Come here," Rai growled as he lunged at her. Suddenly he stopped and fell to the ground holding his crotch.

"I warned you not to come any closer." Nina raced toward the door and quickly down the hall. Her eyes scanned everywhere. Where was she? Was this a strange kind of airplane? She continued to run down the corridor trying to open each door she passed. She found herself in a large opened space, but there was no one here. She spotted where another corridor was, she hurried to it. When she reached the end there was a set of doors. She slowly opened the doors then froze.

"You are not supposed to be here."

"What…you…can talk?" Her mind refused to comprehend what was right in front of her. Two lizard-looking man-things were seated in what appeared to be a cockpit. Her eyes wandered down to the long tail of the one sitting closer to her. The thing's head look like that of a snake, his skin looked like black rubber, but a bit scaly.

"Where is your protector?"

The creature talked to her, but his mouth didn't move.

"Don't be frightened, we are part of the Rundal race."

"There you are." Rai grabbed Nina and carried her back to her quarters then threw her on the bed.

"What the hell were those things?"

"Those were the Rundal, who do you think built this metal beast? They are allies and you would be wise to remember that." Rai walked over to the door. His cock and balls ached from the kick she gave him. "I will be back and I will take what is mine," he growled as he slammed the door shut.

Nina heard him lock the door. "Oh shit…oh shit…" she repeated to herself. This sci-fi crap was really happening. "Deal with it girl," she said as she took a deep breath. Her main concern was keeping Rai off of her. She climbed out of bed and began searching for anything she could use as a weapon. She didn't want to hurt him badly or anything, but there was no way she was going to let him just rape her either.

Chapter 2

"Did you feel that?" Robin asked as she held Demos' hand to her very large belly.

"Niro's son is restless." Demos smiled as he felt the baby moving in Robin's stomach.

"And I am getting restless waiting for his arrival," Niro said as he entered the room.

Demos stood up and stepped away from Robin. Though his gestures were innocent, no warrior wants another male that close to his mate.

Niro walked over to Robin then came down to his knees and gently kissed her rounded belly. "It shouldn't be much longer." He reached up and caressed Robin's face. "You should rest, little one."

"Oh I am fine. What I would like to do is walk around a bit."

"Don't wander too far."

"Yeah, yeah, now help me up."

Niro gently helped her up. "Don't …"

"I know, I know, don't overdue it." She grabbed Niro's arm and pulled him down to her. She kissed him softly then slowly left the room.

Niro watched her leave then turned his attention to Demos. "The baby should arrive any day now. Robin has already carried the baby a week longer than any Malka female has done."

Demos could see the worried look on Niro's face. "Remember your mate is from Earth, so I am sure things are a little different."

"You are right."

"There is more on your mind, isn't there?"

"The Larmat Clan has been pretty quiet this last year, mostly because they have been fighting amongst themselves. Rasmus has secured his place as leader and has united the tribes of the Larmat Clan. My scouts tell me, Rasmus wants Robin and my son dead."

"No one will touch your family, Niro."

"But he will try. Now with Robin so close to giving birth, I fear he will strike now." Niro walked over to the large balcony. "I fear Rasmus will wage war. What better time than when the leader of your enemy is distracted."

"Then we will destroy any enemies that come near our villages."

"I am sending more scouts and have paid handsomely for some Larmat spies. I will find out what Rasmus is up to. But I fear Rasmus has also secured some Dascon spies as well. He is a far cleverer enemy than Malin was."

"I will find these Dascon spies."

"Demos, I have something I want to ask you." Niro turned back around and faced Demos.

"Ask me anything."

"Why did you not go to Earth and pick out a mate for yourself? You did win the Trials last year." Niro had managed to put aside his visions of Demos and Robin being together. He had to offer up Robin as a prize for the Trials Demos had won. But being leader now, he sees Demos as the warrior he is. Demos is strong, skilled and most of all loyal, too valuable an asset to Dascon to let petty jealousy get in the way. Besides, he and Demos go back a long ways.

"I want to protect your mate and unborn child. Though I feel you are a good leader for our people, you have recently taken control. If I help protect what is most precious to you, then you can focus on what you need to do as leader."

"I trust you with my mate's life, Demos." Niro turned back toward the balcony and looked out over the main village of the Dascon Clan. The fact was he did trust Demos and was grateful he could depend on him. "The ship will be back soon from Earth. I would like for you to take a few warriors and escort the new females and their protectors to me."

"Yes Niro."

Niro could hear Demos leave. He now knew why his father Hakan would sometimes just stare out across the village. Being leader of his people was an enormous responsibility. Every decision he made, no matter how small, affected his people. He also knew why his father was reluctant to go to war. The warrior in him was ready for battle, but the leader in him didn't want to send his people off to get killed.

"Niro."

He smiled, feeling Robin's small hand on his back. She was his oasis from it all. Niro turned around and took her gently into his arms.

"You are a good leader, Niro. Your people respect and love you."

Niro kissed the top of her head then led her over to the bed. "You must rest, little one."

"Don't worry about me and your son." Robin rubbed her belly. "Tomar is here to help with the delivery." She sat down on the bed and opened her arms up to Niro. He fell to his knees and laid his head down on her belly. "I will be alright, Niro."

"I hope so, little one. You are my life."

"Niro." Robin gently ran her fingers through his long, dark hair.

ജ്ഞ്ഞ്ഞ

Demos walked down toward where the ship had docked, with two other warriors flanking him. He always walked with such authority that the younger warriors simply moved out of his way as he came by.

Demos bowed his head respectfully at the two Rundal warriors as they passed him.

"I wonder what the Earth females will look like. Niro and Saa's mates are so small and fragile looking, makes me wonder if all Earth women are this way?" one of the warriors asked.

"But they are rather beautiful," the other chimed in.

"Enough!" Demos barked. He saw Samson walking down the corridor with a petite woman beside him. The woman was delicate looking with long brown hair. What Demos really noticed was how frightened the woman looked. She hung close to Samson as if she already trusted him to protect her.

"Samson is liable to hurt the small female," the warrior whispered to the other.

"Samson it is good that you have returned safely." Demos kept his distance from Samson. A Dascon warrior was very protective of his female, especially one that was just named a female's protector. Any warrior that approached the female was assumed that he was challenging her protector.

"This is Jamie and she is my female." Samson glared at Demos and the other two warriors.

"Niro wishes to meet your female."

Samson nodded his head then led Jamie passed the three men.

Demos looked back up the corridor when he heard a woman's voice shouting. He couldn't make out what she was saying, but it was obvious she wasn't happy. He then caught sight of Rai dragging a woman down the corridor by chains he had secured to her wrists. Demos' heart pounded faster as he took in the sight of the woman. She was rather small; her hair was short and a rich brown color. Her body was strong, but yet still very feminine. The closer they got he could make out the brilliant blue color of her eyes. Judging by the way she struggled and seeing how Rai had chained her up, she must have been the one to put the bruises all over Rai. Demos had never seen a female like this before. He expected her to act like the other Earth woman, afraid and confused. But not this female, she was very angry and looked ready to fight even being chained up.

"Oh God damn it," Nina growled, when she saw the other three warriors in front of them. "Alright which one of you is the leader of this testosterone tribe?"

"Niro is our leader," Rai said as he pulled on the chains, dragging her behind him.

"Are you her protector?" Demos asked.

"Yeah, this wild one is mine."

"Excuse me." Nina pulled on her chains trying to get Rai in kicking distance. She looked up at Demos. "You seem to be in charge of something, tell this asshole to unchain me." She couldn't help but admire the way Demos looked. He was big, muscular, just like the other warriors, but it was the way he looked at her that made her body shudder. His face was rather handsome, he had a scar going over one of his eyes, but the other one was the prettiest violet color.

"I am your protector," Rai growled and pulled on her chain, making her lurch forward.

"Niro wants to meet your female."

"Oh good, the leader, well I want to meet him too. And my name is Nina. Stop calling me female." Nina tried to kick Demos.

Demos stepped back a little and was most amused by this female's lack of fear. He followed them as they headed out. Nina walked quietly behind Rai. But she kept looking back at Demos.

Demos' body stirred watching the way her hips would sway as she walked. She wasn't trying to seduce no one and yet she was. Both females had been dressed like the other Malka women already. The silky fabric which was made from the Balma tree, was used to make the garments the women wore. The long gown shimmered in the sunlight, Demos' attention was drawn to the slit that went up the gown, just enough to give him a peek at Nina's well toned leg. His eyes traveled up to her bare shoulders and arms. She was a strong looking woman, almost like the Malka females. Her short shoulder-length brown hair bounced with each step she took.

"Whoa," Nina exclaimed as they exited the building. Never had she seen anything this beautiful as the countryside of Malka. The air was so clear. There were no power lines cluttering up everything. The colors of everything seemed magnified. Beautiful didn't seem accurate enough to describe it. She allowed Rai to escort her to the awaiting carriage. "What an ugly horse." Nina looked at the animal that was hooked to the carriage.

"That is a Bamk," Rai stated.

"Well then, what an ugly Bamk." The thing looked kind of like a horse, but very hairy with two tails and some nasty pointy teeth.

Nina tried to climb into the carriage and was growing frustrated when Rai pulled at her chains. She felt a pair of strong hands on her waist as she was lifted up into the carriage. She heard Rai growl and then he pulled her over to him. Nina sat down and looked across from them and watched as Demos sat down.

"Thank you," she quietly said to Demos, realizing he was the one who helped her into the carriage. She noticed both men wore a golden bracelet on each wrist with strange markings on them. "What are those symbols of?" she asked, pointing to the markings on Rai's bracelet.

"This is a symbol of my Clan," Rai said, pointing to the marking that looked like a dragon. "And this is the mark of my family." He pointed at the symbol that almost looked like a "s".

"What about you?" Nina pointed at Demos' wrist. "Show me your family mark."

Rai grew angry when Demos lifted his wrist up so Nina could inspect his bracelet.

Nina looked at the symbol on Demos' bracelet that looked like a pair of wings.

"You are my female, it is not wise to talk with other males." Rai pulled on her chain.

"Oh get over yourself. I will talk to whoever I want to."

"No you won't. I am your protector, damn it, and you have no choice but to listen to me."

"Really? We will see about that." Nina lurched to the side as Rai pulled at her chain harder this time.

"You must be careful with your female," Demos growled.

"I am not hurting her. Are you challenging me Demos?"

"Can you two put this macho bullshit away for awhile?" Nina sighed and looked out the window. Malka was beautiful, there was no denying that. Nina gasped seeing the large village nestled in a valley with a huge mountain range just beyond it. The closer they got she could see two very big towers that seemed to shimmer in the light as if they were made of jewels. She watched the men walked down the streets of the village. All of them were dressed like Demos and Rai, all of them muscular and rather handsome. The few women she did see were dressed like her. A small group of children were waving at the carriage. Demos waved back while Rai simply sat there as if he was lost in thought.

When they passed the two towers she saw in the distance earlier, Nina could see that in fact the towers had all sorts of jewels covering them. The large building they pulled up to had to be where the leader was. Nina for the first time since they arrived started to get nervous.

Rai pulled her out of the carriage and escorted her toward two large wooden doors. Men carrying spears opened the doors and allowed them to pass.

"Leader hut," Rai quietly said to her as they walked down the hall.

The walls were made of fine wood in different color veneers. The floor was made of stone but sparkled like the towers did. The furniture was made of wood and had some sort of fur covering them. She couldn't help but noticed the large crystals hanging on the walls, which seemed to be a source of light.

They were escorted to a rather large room, which looked to be some sort of meeting place. Nina saw Jamie, she briefly met her on the ship. She watched as the warriors, who were inside the chamber, bowed their heads.

"Rai and Samson I am glad to see you have arrived safely." Niro extended his hand toward Robin as she entered the room. "Please introduce your females to me."

"This is Jamie and the other is Rai's female Nina."

"Jamie and Nina greetings, my name is Niro and I am the leader of the Dascon clan. This is my mate Robin and she will help you to adjust. Why is Nina in chains?" Niro just noticed the woman was bound.

"To protect her, Niro."

"From what?"

"From me having to subdue her when she attacks me."

"Unchain her," Robin spoke up.

Everyone was surprised when they heard the sound of a sword being unsheathed. "I challenge you Rai," Demos growled.

Samson moved Jamie and Nina out of the way and Niro placed himself in front of Robin.

"What?" Rai looked strange as he unsheathed his sword.

"I want your female."

Niro watched as the two men circled each other. Demos lunged for Rai missing him, but Rai fell to the ground anyways.

"I admit defeat, the female is yours," Rai said, releasing his sword.

"I think he…gave up a little easy," Robin said as she held onto Niro's arm.

Demos sheathed his sword and looked at Rai lying there. This has never happened before that a warrior gave up so easy. Rai obviously wanted to be rid of his female. Demos walked over to Nina and looked for a way to unchain her. "Where is the key?"

Rai handed him up the key and Demos quickly unchained Nina.

"Okay just what in the hell happened?" Nina said, rubbing her wrist.

"I am your protector now."

"What?"

"Demos is your protector now, you little conja. I don't know why you want such a female Demos, but you are welcome to her. Niro…" Rai stood up and turned toward Niro. "I want another female. I am the winner of the Trials therefore it's my right."

"I will see what can be done."

"You will take back your insult of my female or I will run my blade through you," Demos growled.

Nina looked at Demos standing their ready to fight for her honor. She had no idea what a conja was, but apparently it wasn't something good. Right now she didn't know what to think. The only thing she knew is that woman standing behind the leader of these barbarians was very pregnant and these big oafs shouldn't be fighting so close to her. "Hey knock it off already. I don't really care what that ox thinks of me anyways."

"He insulted you and he will apologize."

"Rai unless you want to fight Demos, I strongly suggest you apologize," Niro added. He slowly backed Robin up to the far end of the room.

Nina was surprised when Rai drew his sword. "You have got to be kidding me. You two are really going to slice at each other."

"Quiet female," Demos growled at her.

"Don't tell me to be quiet. I want you both to stop this."

"Nina come here," Niro said as he drew his sword.

"Come on Nina," Robin said.

Nina went over toward Robin. Someone had to watch out for this poor pregnant lady. Hell she could get hurt. "Aren't you going to stop them?" Nina looked up at Niro. Damn the leader of these guys was pretty darn hot, she couldn't help but think. His green eyes sparkled like emeralds and his lips were so full they begged to be kissed. He was just as big and muscular as the other guys and all of them had long dark hair. Nina shook her head and snapped herself out of it. "Aren't you going to stop this?" she repeated.

"It is not my concern," Niro replied as he kept his eyes on the two men.

Demos circled Rai and waited for him to attack first.

"Oh damn it, your wife or mate or whatever she is called is very pregnant. She shouldn't be so close to their little quarrel."

"Demos is protecting your honor female. You should be grateful he is willing to challenge Rai."

"Grateful?"

"Shh," Robin grabbed Nina's hand. "Thank you for your concern of my welfare, but I know Niro won't let any harm come to me. You must calm down so Demos can focus on his fight."

"They could kill each other with those damn swords."

"They might do just that, so you need to be quiet." Robin gently pulled Nina back toward her.

Nina looked over at the two men when she heard the sound of swords clashing. There was no way they would really kill each other, was there? She held her breath as Demos attacked Rai. Until finally he pinned Rai under him with his sword at Rai's neck.

"Now, I have truly won the right to be her protector. You will apologize to my female or I will slice your throat." Demos pushed the point of his sword firmly to Rai's neck.

"I apologize female." Rai swallowed hard. "You are the better warrior Demos."

Demos climbed off Rai and then helped him to his feet. "You fought well," he said.

Rai nodded his head then left the room.

"You were going to kill him weren't you?" Nina charged over to Demos.

"If he hadn't apologized, yes I would have."

"I don't believe this. I don't even know what in the hell a conja is, so needless to say I wasn't insulted. Don't do that again." Nina was growing angrier by the moment. "And you leader, Niro I believe that was your name. Tell me why you took me and Jamie from Earth. And took is the right word here. What in the hell gave you the right to do that?"

"I am sorry that you were taken from your home. But my people need more females or our race will die out. You will not be harmed, I swear it, especially with Demos as your protector."

Nina sank to her knees as the gravity of her situation hit her. She was stuck here, wherever here was. What in the hell was she going to do?

"It is alright?" Demos looked down at her, not quite sure what to do. He wanted to take her into his arms and try to bring her some comfort, but he wasn't sure if that was the right thing to do at this moment.

"Why don't you two leave your females with me. I will explain everything to them," Robin said.

Samson nodded his head toward Robin then gently caressed Jamie's hair. She turned to him as if she was a frightened child. "I will not be far." He smiled down to her. He loved the fact she saw him as her protector already. He couldn't help but feel sorry for Demos. Nina was going to be a real pain in the butt. But more so having your female reject you must be very painful. The way Nina is acting she is liable to do just that to poor Demos.

"Alright." Jamie's voice was soft.

"Would you like that?" Demos asked.

"You mean you are actually asking my permission?" Nina said quietly.

"Do you wish me to leave?"

"Yes."

Demos bowed his head toward Niro and Robin then left the room. He stood outside just beyond the door. He didn't know what possessed him to challenge Rai for the troublesome female. He just knew he wanted her. He slowly slid down the wall and came to a seated position. He leaned his head back against the wall. His body ached to have Nina, but he wouldn't force her to be with him. Did Rai force her? Or did she manage to fight him off. Judging by the bruises all over Rai, he had a feeling she fought him off. This brought a smile to Demos' face. Her fire drew him to her, but it was the same fire he feared would keep him away. Would she accept him as her protector? Demos closed his eyes. Let her get adjusted first then he would try to claim her.

Chapter 3

Robin led the women to the room just off of the meeting chamber. "I was from Earth too," she said as she gestured for the two women to sit down.

"You were?" Nina asked.

"Yep, so was Sabrina. You will meet her later."

"Now would be a good time to get the hell out of here," Nina said to Jamie.

"And go where?" Robin smiled at the small male who brought them some drinks.

Nina watched the male leave the room. "You mean not all the men here are big and beefy?"

"No, the smaller ones are called weaker males."

"Oh that is stupid, why are they called that?"

"Because they are treated as though they are less than a male. Here let me explain something. There is a severe shortage of women on Malka. A strange illness wiped out a lot of them, then a war between the two clans didn't help matters. Malka warriors are a rather horny bunch of men, for the lack of a better way to put that. And with too few females to go around, well...the weaker males are used like women."

"Oh that is a bunch of crap. Just because some dude isn't all buffed he has to be fucked by the bigger ones." Nina made a sigh noise then rolled her eyes. "Let me guess, he who is the strongest wins on this planet."

"Yeah, pretty much. I didn't like the way the weaker males are treated and have talked to Niro about this.

But until there are enough females for the warriors there really isn't anything Niro can do."

"When are you due?" Jamie asked as she sipped the tasty tea.

"Any day now."

"You are having twins?" Nina asked.

"No just one big boy." Robin chuckled, rubbing her belly.

"There has to be a way to go back to Earth. Wouldn't you like to go home too?" Nina asked.

"Niro is my home. Wherever he goes I go. Besides, Malka isn't a bad place to live."

"Sure, if you are a muscled bound warrior dude. They had no right just to kidnap us like this."

"Did you have someone back on Earth? Is that why you want to go back to Earth so bad? If it is maybe I can talk to Niro and…"

Nina held her hand up to stop Robin. "Actually, I didn't have shit back on Earth. But that isn't the point." Nina sighed and sat back into her chair. She really didn't have anything to go back to. But still…Nina felt her tears start to fill her eyes. Not now, damn it, she repeated to herself. She hated to look weak. She always managed to keep herself from crying, but this whole situation…

"Hey it's okay." Robin stood up and walked over to Nina. She slowly sat down next to her. "I understand how you feel in a way. But the moment I touched Niro I knew I wanted to stay with him."

"I feel that way about Samson," Jamie added. "I can't explain it. At first I was so scared, hell I still am. But, Samson has been so gentle with me and…" Jamie blushed a little. "I have never been made love to like the way Samson did to me."

"You mean you have already…oh hell, I had to fight off that oaf Rai the whole trip over here."

"He didn't rape you did he?" Robin asked.

"No, but it wasn't from a lack of trying."

"How did you manage to fight him off?" Robin was very intrigued.

"I am a black belt in karate. So that fucker wasn't touching me if I could help it." Nina smiled when she heard Robin and Jamie start to laugh.

"Once I have my baby, you will have to teach me a few moves. I know Sabrina would love to learn as well."

"Did someone mention my name?" Sabrina hurried over to Robin and rubbed her belly. "Damn girl, when are you going to have this baby already?"

"Sabrina, this is Nina and Jamie. They are from Earth."

"Oh, fellow captives, it's nice to meet you." Sabrina shook their hands then sat down next to Jamie. "I am Saa's mate. See here you have to introduce yourself that way. It keeps all the horny warriors away from you."

Nina smiled. She was starting to feel a little better. Robin and Sabrina seemed nice, but more importantly they seemed happy. "When is your baby due?"

"Not for a few months yet. Oh Robin, I just found out from Tomar that me and Saa are having a little girl."

"Oh, that is wonderful news. I can't wait to tell Niro."

"Don't worry, Saa is already telling him."

"Who is Tomar?" Nina asked.

"He is the leader of the Rundal and a very skilled doctor."

"Rundal? Those lizard-looking things?"

"You have seen a Rundal already?" Robin asked.

"Yeah, on the airplane…spaceship thing."

"Lizard-looking things?" Jamie looked nervous.

"Oh don't worry honey, they look like lizard people, but they are the gentlest and sweetest race of beings there is." Sabrina grabbed a cup of tea. "So, have you two been with your protectors?" She took a sip of her tea. "I see by Jamie's blush that's a yep, what about you Nina?"

"Uh…no, and I don't plan to be with my protector." Nina made the sign of quotes with her fingers when she said protector.

"Really? You know Jamie you should tell Nina just how skilled a Malka warrior is with his cock and not to mention the size of his cock. Oh damn I thought Saa's cock was going to rip me in two the first time he fucked me. Mmmm, just thinking about his big cock makes me all tingly."

Jamie blushed even more.

"Oh, I see that Samson's cock is pretty big and…ah, talented," Sabrina teased Jamie.

"Oh for Pete sakes. Okay I admit these warriors are pretty darn hot, but still…" Nina didn't know how to finish the sentence. Images of Demos standing there with his sword drawn ready to protect her honor wouldn't leave her mind. Neither would his face, the way he looked at her made her feel so…beautiful. But this was silly to have these thoughts. For Christ sakes, she was a grown woman not some smitten schoolgirl.

"Nina, Demos is a good man. You are lucky," Robin said.

"Lucky am I. Yep, being kidnapped and brought to the planet of beef cake was high on my list of things I wanted to do."

"You are only going to make it harder on yourself. If you are still unhappy when the Rundal go back to Earth I will ask Niro to let you go with them. But enjoy your time here, you might find it was what you have been looking for." Robin stood up. "I am feeling really tired right now, I will let Sabrina show you back to your protectors. We can talk more later."

"Do you need some help?" Nina jumped up.

"Oh no, I am just fine, carrying this little guy around just tires me out pretty fast. It was nice meeting both of you and please feel free to come and talk to me whenever you would like."

"Okay ladies, let me escort you back to your men, and speaking of men…hey baby." Sabrina opened her arms to Saa. "Ladies, this is my mate Saa. Pretty hot isn't he?"

Saa nodded his head toward the women.

"This is Demos and Samson's females." Sabrina kissed Saa sweetly then turned her attention back toward the women.

Nina looked at Saa, he was bigger than Demos, he had dark hair and eyes, his face was handsome but he had a fierce look about him. Nina watched as this big man rubbed Sabrina's belly gently. She could see the love he had for his woman and their unborn child, Niro had this same look when he was with Robin. Somehow this warmed Nina's heart. But it also confused her. Rai wasn't gentle and sure the hell wasn't very kind. He just wanted to fuck her and nothing more. She didn't know Demos long enough to judge what kind of man he was.

"Come Jamie." Samson quickly went to her and escorted her out of the room.

"Nina." Demos' voice was very deep, something she hadn't really noticed before.

She turned toward him. He stood in the doorway with his arms crossed in front of his chest.

"You better go girl. Remember don't go anywhere without Demos." Sabrina gently nudged Nina forward.

"Why not?"

"He is your protector." Sabrina led Nina off to the side. "There are a lot, and I mean a lot, of horny men on this planet. They would have no trouble with raping you to satisfy their lust. Besides that, there are some really strange creatures on this planet too. Trust me, don't leave Demos' side." Sabrina gave Nina a gentle but firm shove toward Demos.

Nina slowly walked over to him. She was startled when she felt his hand caressed her cheek. This caused her to back away from him.

"I will take you to our chamber where you can rest." Demos turned around and started to walk out. Nina followed him. He kept looking back to make sure she was following him.

They said nothing as they made their way to his chamber. Niro allowed only the finest warriors to live in the leader hut. Demos opened the door and allowed her to step in.

"Sleep Nina."

"I am a bit tired." She turned to him. "Where do you sleep?"

"Beside you."

"Ummm, I don't think so." She could see the strange look on his face. She couldn't make out if he was shocked, hurt or angry.

"I will leave and let you rest." Demos stomped out of the room. He locked the door. He was hurt and angry. Why was this woman being so difficult? She didn't even want to share his bed. He headed out toward the training grounds. He needed to work off his anger and not to mention he had to distract himself. He wanted her so badly, but she appeared not to want him. How much longer was he going to be able to hold off his lust before he just took her? He didn't want her against her will, but…. "Arrrgghh!!!" he growled as he hastened his steps toward the training grounds.

Chapter 4

Rasmus thrust harder into the writhing woman under him. He wanted to bury his cock deeper and deeper into her.

"You like that don't you?" he growled as he thrust harder.

"Oh yes, yes, yes Rasmus," Safon cried out as she wrapped her long legs around him.

"That's it, come for me." Rasmus looked down into her face as she climaxed. "Yeah, that's a good girl." He sped up his thrusting until he finally orgasm.

Both of them were sweating and breathing hard as he laid down on her. "Good girl." He kissed her on the cheek then rolled off.

"I am glad you are pleased." She snuggled down next to him.

Safon was his favorite female. She was so eager to please but yet, she wasn't afraid of him like the others were. He twirled a strand of her golden hair as his mind raced. Niro's mate was due to have her baby any day now. He wanted to kill Robin before she gave birth, but no matter, one way or the other Niro's mate and son will be dead. But he knew how Niro thought and getting close to Niro's family would prove most difficult. Rasmus looked down at Safon, then at the strand of her golden hair that was wrapped around his finger.

"Would you do anything for me?" he asked.

"You know I would."

"Then get dressed and follow me." Rasmus climbed out of bed and tied on his loincloth. He grabbed his sword and placed it into its sheath then strapped it to his back. He turned to see if Safon was ready. She had quickly gotten dressed and was already behind him. Rasmus smiled then headed out of the room. He made his way to the dressing chamber of his females. Unlike Dascon males who had only one female per male, the Larmat males could have many. The more power a male had, the more females he was allowed. Since Rasmus was the leader of the Larmat Clan he had ten females. He often times would allow his best warriors to play with his females. This kept them loyal and eager to please.

"Safon I want you to dye your hair the color of a Dascon female." Rasmus grabbed a dark-haired female and pulled her to him. "Just like this."

"Yes Rasmus." Safon bowed her head. Though she had no desire to look like one of those Dascon sluts, she would do anything for Rasmus.

She waited for Rasmus to leave then she went to the Dascon female. "You heard him, make my hair as ugly as yours."

The Dascon females who were unlucky enough to get captured by the Larmat warriors lived a dreadful existence. They were looked upon as just objects, not even human. Escape was difficult, but it fueled the wills of many of the captive females.

Rasmus waited patiently in his chambers. His thoughts drifted to Niro, and how much he wanted the lands of the Dascon Clan. The Rundal were the allies of the Dascon. The efforts of Malin, the former leader of the Larmat, to wipe out this race of beings was futile. Niro protected the Rundal. Unlike Malin, Rasmus wanted the knowledge of the Rundal. If he destroyed Niro and took over the Dascon Clan, the Rundal would have no choice but to aid the Larmat people or face certain annihilation. Another warrior's name kept drifting into his consciousness, Demos. Rasmus growled just thinking about him. Niro would have died that day he came to save his mate Robin, would have and should have if Demos didn't save him. But it was more than that, Rasmus had fought Demos before. It seemed like ages ago. Both of them novice warriors, but still he managed to mark Demos with his blade, blinding him in that one eye, every time Rasmus saw Demos' scar it reminded him of his failure. He should have killed Demos that day, but who knew what inner strength Demos had. Any other warrior who sustained such an injury would have been easy to defeat, but Demos fought on forcing Rasmus to retreat. Rasmus remembered the beating his father gave him, that was the last time that bastard of a father touched him. Rasmus killed him a week later, freeing his mother from the abuse his father gave both of them. Rasmus could feel the anger build the more he thought of his past. Demos reminded him of that past and he wanted more than anything to kill this reminder.

"Rasmus." Safon's soft voice brought him out of his memories.

"Perfect." He smiled. Safon's hair was now a rich dark brown. The bark of the Balma tree mixed with various roots was used to make the dye. He wasn't sure if it would work on human hair, seeing how it was used to dye the hair of the Bamk. The Bamk's hair was dyed dark to help camouflage them from the wild conjas.

"Now I want you to listen carefully, Safon. What I ask of you is most important."

She came to him and sat down by his feet and looked up at him, giving him her full attention.

"You are going to pretend you have escaped from here. You will make your way to the Dascon village. Niro will no doubt take pity on you and have you sheltered in his hut for your safety. Once you have gained Niro's confidence he will allow you to be around his mate Robin. You must time this well because you will have only one chance at it. When you feel the moment is right you will kill Robin. But my favorite, I must warn you Robin will be protected, no doubt by Demos, so you will have to find a way to get him to drink this." Rasmus motioned to the servant boy who quickly came over and handed him a small vile of liquid.

"What is that Rasmus?"

"This is from the root of the safon plant which you are named after." He smiled down at her. "Put this liquid into something Demos will drink. It will make him unable to move. Make him watch you kill Robin."

"Then I will kill Demos for you."

"No, let him live. Niro will kill him for failing to protect Robin." Rasmus stroked her dark hair. "Do this for me my favorite and I will make you my mate."

"It will be done. But Rasmus, though I don't wish to ask this I must."

"Go ahead."

"I will have to be raped by at least two warriors. You have been very kind to me and my body has no marks on it. Niro may not believe my story."

"You are very clever." Though Rasmus didn't wish for any harm to come to her, she did have a point. "I don't wish to witness this or see any evidence of the brutality you will suffer. You will leave tomorrow." Rasmus pulled her up to him and kissed her softly. "Return to me, I want you to bare my children."

"Nothing will keep me from you." She kissed him again.

He got up and headed for the door. He took one last look at her then left the room. He summoned two of his biggest warriors. His heart was heavy as he instructed them to rape Safon.

Chapter 5

Nina stretched as she slowly awoke. The large bed she was snuggled in was very comfortable. It took her a moment to realize were she was. She sat up and looked around for Demos, but he was nowhere in sight. She heard the sound of water running in the other room. She slowly got up. She made sure she was dressed. She would have to remember to ask Robin for some more clothes. She was surprised to see a large variety of long wrap dresses hung up against the wall. She ran her hands over the silky fabric of each beautiful garment. She would have to thank Robin for her kindness. Nina smiled and walked over to the next room.

"Oh…" she whispered as she watched Demos remove his loincloth and slowly emerge himself into the large pool of water. He ducked under the water and quickly came back up. His long ebony hair was slick back from his face. She didn't really noticed how long his hair was before, but it hung down the length of his back. He and the other warriors always seemed to have their hair tied back. She couldn't resist watching him bathe himself, though she knew she should give him his privacy. Her eyes watched the droplets of water as they ran down his broad muscular chest. He was a gorgeous man she had to give him that.

"You can join me if you wish." Demos' deep voice startled her.

"Ah…umm... ah... oh shit." Nina hurried back into the bed chamber. She was a bit annoyed that the door was locked. She wanted to get the hell out of this chamber. She was so embarrassed, she felt like a pervert or something. She could hear the sounds of Demos climbing out of the bathing pool. "Oh great." She bit her lip and tried to think of anything that would explain why she was watching him in his private moment.

"What is wrong?" he said as he entered the bedchamber.

"Nothing. Oh, I have to thank Robin for the clothes," she said quickly.

"Then you like them?"

"Very much so."

"I am pleased to hear that. I bought those for you and wasn't sure if you would like my choices."

"You bought them…well…thank you." She slowly looked up. He was standing only a few feet away from her. That look in his eyes began to make her body react.

"Nina." Demos slowly walked over to her. He wanted her so badly that he had to take deep breaths to calm himself; otherwise he might force her to be with him.

"Look, I don't want to be stuck in this room all day." She looked up again, he was standing right next to the bed. Her eyes wandered down and saw exactly what was on his mind by that large bulge he had in his loincloth.

"I want to be with you. Will you allow it?"

"No…just stay over there." She stood up and went to the door.

"I won't hurt you."

"That's not the point. I don't know you."

"My body is yours to do with whatever you like."

"That's a nice offer, but I will have to pass on that."

"Why are you resisting me? Do you not find me pleasing?" Demos' hand went up to the scar on his face. "Is this why you refuse me?"

"No…you are a very handsome man."

"Then why do you refuse me? I will be a good protector to you."

"I am sure you would be more than capable to protect me. But I don't need your protection, okay."

"Don't need or don't want." Demos was starting to get angry. He could see by her erect nipples and the way she looked at his body that she wanted him, then why was she refusing him?

"I don't want to argue with you, just unlock the door so I can leave this chamber."

"No."

"Excuse me."

"No, I am your protector and I will claim you as mine." He hurried over to the door and grabbed her. He was surprised by her kick. The kick was solid enough to knock him into the bed. He sat up and grabbed her with both hands this time. He pulled her onto the bed with him. He groaned when she kneed him on the thigh.

"Rrrrrr…" he growled as he pinned her under him and raised her arms above her head. She was trapped, though she continued to struggle under him.

"Let me go damn it."

"I am going to claim you, Nina." He pinned her arms using one hand then used the other to rip at her dress. He looked at her exposed breasts then cupped one in his hand.

"Stop it!!! Get off me!!" She continued to struggle under him. She never felt so powerless before. She managed to fight off Rai, but she couldn't seem to get Demos off of her.

He pulled at her dress hungry to see more of her body. His cock ached and he felt the sexual frenzy beginning to take over. She would be his, she couldn't stop him now.

"Demos please don't," she sobbed.

Demos' breath caught. He looked into her beautiful face the fear and sadness he saw in her eyes tore at him, calming his frenzy. "Nina...I am sorry." He let go of her hands and climbed off of her. He grabbed one of the furs and wrapped her in it. "I am so sorry." He went to touch her, to wipe away the tears that stained her beautiful face.

"Don't touch me," she quietly said as she turned her face from him.

He couldn't stop himself, he pulled her into his arms and gently held her. He would prove that he could be gentle. She didn't fight him this time. "I am sorry, Nina." He felt her melt into him, he held her tighter.

"Please leave me alone for awhile."

Demos let her go and climbed out of the bed. "I will leave the door unlocked, but I will stand guard. You mustn't go anywhere without me. It is not safe."

Nina wrapped the furs tighter around her. She would have to learn more about this world if she hoped to survive in it. She wasn't going back home. She would have to accept that if she wished to adapt to her new world. That was the one thing she was good at, adapting. She took a deep breath to calm herself. Demos didn't rape her, he could have very easily. This scared her, she had always been able to fend for herself. But he did stop...Nina shook her head, she didn't want to think about it anymore. She went over to the gowns Demos bought her. She smiled a little, she couldn't help it, especially when she saw the vials of perfume, and hell, a whole little vanity was set up for her. He did all of this for her. When did he have time? It must have been when she was sleeping. No one had ever done anything like this before for her. She closed her eyes and centered herself. There was no point getting all choked up over Demos' act of generosity. She carefully got ready. Her hands lovingly touched each bottle of perfume. She could almost imagine Demos' big hands touching the delicate bottles trying to decide which one she might like. She looked at herself in the mirror. The beautiful silver dress covered her but yet, gave glimpses of her body. She didn't really wear that many dresses before, saw no need to. The men she went out with didn't really take her anywhere that warrants wearing a dress. She felt beautiful wearing this silky garment. "Well enough of this," she said. She had to find Robin and start learning about Malka.

She saw Demos standing off to the side of the door as she exited the room.

"You are so beautiful, Nina." He smiled at her.

She liked his smile. She noticed he had dimples, which gave him a boyish charm. "Thank you."

"Where are you going?"

"I want to talk with Robin if she isn't too busy today."

"Let me escort you to her."

Nina simply nodded her head. She walked beside him, she noticed he slowed down his steps so she could comfortably keep up with him. He led her to a large chamber where she spotted Robin relaxing on a large chair with her feet propped up. Nina couldn't help but smile seeing Niro fuss over her.

"Demos, what's wrong?" Niro stood at attention.

"Nothing, Nina just wanted to spend time with Robin. That's if she is up to company."

"Oh, that would be great." Robin smiled over to Nina.

"Little one, you need to rest." Niro squatted down so he could look Robin in the eyes.

"Oh, stop fussing over me already. A little company is just what I need. Now go on and do your leader stuff."

"Alright, but I will just be in the next chamber if you need me."

Nina could see the love those two had for each other and it caused her a moment of pain. She had never been loved like that. Sure she has had several lovers, but not one ever looked at her the way Niro looked at Robin. Nina glanced up at Demos, he too was watching the loving exchange between Niro and Robin. He sighed and looked down at the ground and for a brief moment, Nina wondered if he had the same thought she just did.

"Come sit by me Nina." Robin gestured to the chair next to her. "Demos I am sure you won't mind if me and Nina have some girl talk. I promise she won't leave the room."

"Would you like that Nina?" he asked.

"Yes." She watched as Demos followed Niro into the next chamber.

"So now what is it you would like to discuss?" Robin adjusted the pillows Niro had placed under her legs.

"Well, I need to know more about Malka. Like what are these dangers Demos keeps talking about? Why do I need his constant protection?"

"Sabrina told me she explained to you about the horny warriors. This is the main threat you will have. I am lucky that Niro is a kind and good man. Some of these Dascon warriors are not, though they are far better than the Larmat warriors."

"Larmat warriors?"

"The Larmat are the Dascon's enemy. They are another danger Demos will protect you from. But, I have yet to see any of them reach this village. Then you have the Conjas. These, umm let's see…well they are basically dragons. That's the closest thing to them. The domestic ones are very useful and are a form of air transportation. But the wild ones will and have killed many people on Malka."

"Dragons?"

"You can ask Demos to show you his Conja, all higher ranking warriors have one."

"So that son of a bitch Rai was calling me a dragon lady."

Robin started to laugh. "Yeah, I guess he was."

"What is so funny?"

"It's just now you know why Demos was so angry at Rai."

"Oh, alright." Nina grabbed a cup of tea and handed it to Robin. "Hey what is your name?" she asked the small male who was serving them tea.

"Laigne," he quietly answered.

"Hello Laigne, my name is Nina." She extended her hand but he backed away very quickly and looked as though he was about to throw up as he nervously scanned the room.

"What?" Nina looked around the room too, trying to see what was freaking out Laigne.

"He is looking for Demos. Thank you Laigne, why don't you see to Sabrina and when you get a chance could you bring us some fruit? I am getting a little hungry." Robin smiled at him and let him make a quick exit.

"Why would he be doing that?"

"Because you talked to him and he was afraid Demos would have been angry about that."

"I don't understand."

"Dascon warriors are a very jealous bunch of guys, so they don't like any male even the weaker ones talking to their women. Now once you are joined, then as long as the woman talks to a man first it's okay for him to speak to her."

"Joining?"

"It is like being married. I will explain that later after you have had time to adjust."

"This sucks, I don't like being told who I can talk to, where I can go."

"It is only to protect you."

"Well it still sucks."

"Nina may I ask you a question?"

"Sure."

"Have you allowed Demos to claim you yet?"

"Claim me, oh you mean fuck me yet?"

"No, I mean claim you. He has to take you as a protector would to establish that you are his. This of course doesn't stop other males from challenging him to be your protector, but it does strengthen the bond between you two."

"He tried…" Nina looked down at her cup of tea. "But he stopped when I asked him too. Rai didn't, he just kept trying until I hurt him bad enough, then he would stop. But he kept trying and trying." She looked up at Robin. "Rai wasn't trying to claim me, he was trying to rape me. But…" She looked back down.

"Demos is not like Rai, Nina. He is a good man. I am going to share something with you." Robin sat her tea down then sat up. "Once a year the Dascon tribe has a big festival they call the Trials. Here warriors compete in several events to show off their skills. The winner of the Trials gets a female as a prize for a night, but also he automatically has the right to choose any new female to be the protector of. Demos won the Trials a year ago and I was the prize."

"What? Ah, didn't Niro have a problem with that?"

"Yes, Niro didn't want to do this, but his father Hakan, who was the leader at the time, insisted. He said it would show Niro's love for his people. Hakan had given his mate Kelila as prize before for this same reason. I was so scared when I was in that room waiting for Demos to take me. I had no choice, if I refused him, I would have shamed Niro. But Demos was gentle, he was eager, but gentle. When I asked him not to do certain things he respected my wishes. I was lucky, because he didn't have to listen to me, he was free to do whatever he wanted with me."

"You slept with Demos!" Nina felt an unexpected pang of jealousy.

Robin waited for Nina to absorb what she had said. When it looked as though Nina had calm down, Robin continued, "Demos has watched over me during my pregnancy allowing Niro to focus on getting use to being leader of the Dascon clan. I have watched Demos defend other females from protectors who felt it is alright to abuse their female. He has never claimed a female for himself, ever. So needless to say when he challenged Rai for you I was stunned. Nina…" Robin reached over and grabbed her hand. "What I am saying is please don't hurt Demos. I know adjusting to Malka is hard, but you have one of the best men to help you adjust. He must feel something for you since he wants to be your protector. Give him a chance."

Nina didn't really know what to say. Give Demos a chance. That was a lot to ask of her. How many other men have she given her heart too, just to have them break it? Now she guards her heart well. She wasn't ready to give it to anyone, much less some barbarian who insisted on treating her as though she was helpless. She was far from helpless. But still that look in his eyes when she refuses him.

"That is a beautiful gown you have on." Robin quickly changed the subject to lighten the mood. The silver gown Nina had on was stunning.

"Oh, thank you."

"Where did you get it? I will have to have my dress maker make me one."

"I don't know. Demos got it for me."

"He did, oh that's sweet."

"So, what is there to do around here, besides dodging the horny males, dragons and the enemy?" Nina chuckled.

Chapter 6

Rai was growing angrier by the moment. Niro told him that he would have to wait for a female due to the way he treated Nina. Rai knew this was Robin's doing. He won the Trials damn it, having a female was his right. Now Niro dared to tell him he had to wait.

Rai stomped down the corridor toward his chambers when Laigne caught his eye. He growled and headed right toward the small male. As expected Laigne dropped the tray of fruit he was carrying and tried to flee from Rai.

"I have plans for you Robin's little bitch servant." Rai grabbed Laigne by the arm and dragged him to his chamber.

"Please Rai, what have I done to anger you so much?"

"You have done nothing, but the one you serve has." Rai threw Laigne into his chamber. "I would hurt her if I could, but I don't wish to feel Niro's anger." Rai grabbed Laigne by the neck and lifted him into the air. "If you tell Niro what I have said I will gut you like a Trof." Rai smiled hearing the gasping noise coming from Laigne, then he let him drop to the ground.

"I will not say anything," Laigne gasped as he backed away from Rai.

"My cock aches, come here and relieve me." Rai removed his loincloth and slowly stroked his cock. "Now you little bitch servant!"

Laigne quickly crawled over to Rai then came up to his knees. He took Rai's cock into his mouth and began to suck.

"All of it, yeah…" Rai grabbed a handful of Laigne's hair as he thrust his cock deeply into Laigne's throat. "Choke on it bitch, for all I care." He chuckled as Laigne struggled, but Rai had a firm grip on his head. "That's it, suck my cock. This is all you are good for weaker male. You are not strong enough to defend our lands, are you?" Rai pulled out his cock. "Are you?"

"No, Rai, I am not skilled with a sword."

"Lick the head of my cock. I want to watch you." Rai watched as Laigne's tongue rolled over the head then down the shaft. He did this over and over, briefly licking at Rai's balls too. "Oh yes, mmmm, tell me weaker male…" Rai pushed Laigne's face closer as he lapped at his balls. "Tell me how it feels to know you will never fuck a woman, will never have her mouth on your cock. Mmmm, tell me."

"I can't miss what I have never known Rai."

Rai laughed and pulled Laigne's hair so he was licking at the head of Rai's cock again. "Suck my cock." Rai forced his cock down Laigne's throat again. He thrust hard not caring whether Laigne was gagging or not. "Yes, mmm, keep sucking, oh yes suck." Rai thrust faster and faster then he held Laigne's head to him, forcing his cock down Laigne's throat as he orgasm. "Drink my seed, bitch servant." Rai pushed Laigne to the floor. "Don't look so relieved bitch. I am not done with you." Rai stroked his cock making it hard again. "I am going to fuck you like a woman. Bend over this bed and get ready to take my cock up that tight ass."

"Please Rai, I beg of you not to make me do that. Please!" Laigne couldn't bear the pain of having a large warrior's cock in his ass. It was pure torture. He looked up at Rai and felt chills run up his body as he watched a malevolent smile spread across Rai's face.

"Bend over bitch servant." Rai chuckled.

ဆဆဆ

Robin was walking with Nina, Demos was guarding both of them, but he kept his distance to give them a little privacy. Nina seemed to enjoy her afternoon with Robin and this made Demos happy. He smiled watching the women laugh, then he went instantly on guard when he saw Robin stop abruptly. He hurried up toward the women.

"What is wrong?"

"This is Laigne's tray. He was supposed to have brought me and Nina something to eat an hour ago. I assumed he got sidetracked with some other chore since I told him there was no real hurry."

Demos looked around there were only warriors' chambers around. He quickly figured out what probably had happened to Laigne. Though using a house servant for sexual release wasn't done much. "I will find him Robin."

"Please hurry and find him Demos. It's not like him to just drop his tray and leave it lying."

"First I must bring you two to Saa."

"I can watch Robin," Nina offered up.

Demos looked at her for a moment. Though every warrior instinct he had told him to just grab the two women and take them to Saa, he just couldn't with Nina looking at him like that, like she wanted to feel useful or something. Then he remembered Niro was still in the meeting chamber. "Let me escort you back to the meeting chamber at least."

"Okay," Nina said as she grabbed Robin by the arm and they headed back toward the meeting chamber.

Demos waited until they were safely back then he left to find Laigne. Demos searched the chambers of the warriors but couldn't find him. As he was walking up toward Rai's chamber he observed Rai throwing Laigne out of his chamber then slamming the door shut. Laigne was slow to get back up. Demos hurried over to help him, but Laigne quickly tried to crawl away from him.

"You have nothing to fear from me."

"Please, don't use me, please Demos."

"I have never used a weaker male." Demos reached down and helped the small man to his feet. "Where is your chamber?"

"You need not waste time tending to me, Demos."

"Never mind, I will take you to Tomar." Demos lifted Laigne up and threw him over his shoulder. He felt Laigne's whole body tense up. The weaker male was still afraid Demos was going to use him. He seemed to relax as Demos entered the area where the Rundal visitors stayed.

"Demos, it is a pleasure to see you again," Tomar said as he greeted him by the door.

"It is always a pleasure to be in your presence great Tomar." Demos slowly let Laigne down.

"What is wrong with this male?" Tomar looked over Laigne.

"I think he was abused by Rai."

"Oh…" Tomar could see Laigne was afraid of him. He was use to this response. After all to a barbarian, Tomar's appearance was most frightening. His reptilian features did take some getting use to. It did take him some time to get use to the barbarian's grotesque features, all that hair, and they had no scales, or even a tail.

"I don't need any treatment I am fine."

"I will determine that. Please remove your covering."

Demos was shocked when he saw the blood all over Laigne's ass and thigh.

"I know Demos, I can never get use to this sight either. The warrior who done this must've known his large organ would have damage this male this way." Tomar went to work fixing Laigne.

Demos thanked him, then he headed back toward Rai's chamber. He banged on the wooden door until Rai opened it up.

"What is it Demos?"

"You are to never touch Robin's servant again."

"Are you ordering me?"

"No I am telling you." Demos drew his sword. "If you wish to make this a challenge I would be more than happy to oblige."

"Calm down Demos. There are plenty of more bitch servants to play with. I will leave that one alone."

"Why did you pick that servant?" Demos sheathed his sword.

"He was handy. Surely you are not reading something into this are you?"

"Leave Laigne alone," Demos growled as he headed back to the meeting chamber. Something was wrong, he could feel it. Maybe he should just kill Rai, but he would have to get Niro's permission first. Niro wouldn't want one of his better warriors executed just for using a house servant. He opened the door to the meeting chamber then stopped quickly. Nina was showing Robin a few of her karate moves. She had hiked up her covering so she could perform some of the moves. Demos' eyes followed the curves of her legs. His cock started to get extremely hard the more he watched her.

"Demos, did you find Laigne?" Robin asked.

"Yes, he is all right. Tomar is tending to him."

"Tomar…why?"

"Laigne was used by a warrior."

"I don't want to hear anymore." Robin didn't want to think about poor Laigne being used like that.

"Hey, it's alright," Nina said.

"Niro!" Robin called out.

Within seconds Niro entered the chamber. "What is wrong?" He quickly went to her.

"Are you busy with anything important?"

"Nothing is more important than you."

"Will you lay with me for awhile?"

"Of course." Niro helped her up to her feet. "Demos take your female back to your chamber."

"Yes Niro."

Nina watched Niro scoop Robin up in his arms and carried her to a different chamber. "Is she okay?"

"She is upset and wants the comfort of Niro's arms." Demos walked over to Nina. "Come Nina we must go back to my chamber."

Nina said nothing but simply followed Demos. She didn't quite understand what was going on, but she had a pretty good idea. She remembered what Robin said about the weaker males.

Demos let Nina go in first. "What were you showing Robin?" he asked.

"Oh, some of my karate moves, though it's hard to do in this dress."

"Will you show me?"

"You want to see my karate moves, why, you will never let me use any of them."

"Please show me. You must have practiced many years to be able to move your body with such strong movements."

"I have studied for more than ten years. Okay I will show you a couple."

Demos watched as she moved her body. She looked so strong, yet graceful. "Will you be able to take down a warrior my size with those moves?"

"I knocked your ass down with my kick before." Nina smiled at him then charged. Demos was surprised when she flipped him over her shoulder. He landed on the ground with a loud thud. "See, now I can flee." She gasped when he instantly jumped back up into a standing position.

"Good, Nina, very good. You should flee if a warrior is much bigger than you." He smiled when he saw the pleased look on her face. Then it hit him, this is what she wanted. She needed to be independent like a warrior was. His smile widened when he thought, she was his beautiful flower, but his flower had deadly thorns.

"What?" She smiled back at him. She couldn't help herself, his smile was contagious.

"You are very strong female. I am proud of you, my Nina."

My Nina...those words echoed through her head. She was too afraid to admit to herself she liked the way that sounded in his deep voice.

"Thank you," was all she could manage to say.

"Nina..." Demos went to reach for her then pulled his hand away.

Nina's breathing became more erratic when she saw his gesture. He wanted her, hell it showed in his eyes. She wanted him, she couldn't deny it any longer. She looked up at him then reached for the clasp between her breasts that held her covering on. She unhooked it and let her covering fall from her body.

"You are so beautiful," Demos whispered as he moved closer to her.

Nina reached for the ties of his loincloth, she tried to unhook it but her hands shook too much. Demos quickly removed it for her. He groaned when he felt her hand on his cock.

"Whoa, you are a big boy aren't you," she cooed as she dropped to her knees before him and took his cock into her mouth.

"Nina…oh Nina." He gently ran his fingers through her hair. "I need to be inside you." He gently lifted her up. She wrapped her legs around him and eased her pussy down onto his cock. His cock was enormous and it stretched her almost to the point of pain. He leaned her up against the wall as he slowly began to thrust.

"Demos, yes, yes…oh yes," she cried out as he buried his cock to the hilt in her.

She felt her ass bang onto the wall with each one of his powerful thrusts.

"Nina I want to claim you."

She sighed when he pulled his cock out and carried her to the bed. He tossed her onto the bed then positioned her on her hands and knees. Slowly he filled her with his cock again. He thrust harder and harder, growling and grunting. Nina gasped when she felt him bite her shoulder pinning her under him. There was something so primal, so animalistic about the way he took her. His deep low growls made her body shiver as he thrust harder and deeper into her.

"You are my female," he roared, "say it, tell me you are mine."

"Demos," she sighed.

"Say it," he growled as he bit her shoulder again.

"I am your female!" she screamed as her orgasm engulfed her.

"I am your male, no other male will touch you, say it," he growled biting her shoulder again.

"You are my…male," she could barely get out.

"YESSS!!!" he cried out as he arched up and enjoyed his strong orgasm. He continued to thrust until the last of his seed was in her. He slowly pulled his cock out of her and lay down in the bed taking her with him. He held her tightly to him. He breathed in her scent, listened to the quiet sound of her breathing and felt her heartbeat. It felt so right lying here with her cradled in his arms. Did she feel the same way about him, probably not, but right now everything was perfect. He pulled her closer and held her tightly to him.

Nina lay there surrounded by the warmth of his strong body. It felt right, so very right being with him. Any resistance she had left was gone at this moment. He did more than claim her body, he had claimed her heart and she knew, hell she could feel it. She inhaled deeply and just melted into his embrace.

Chapter 7

Demos couldn't be happier as he showed Nina around the village. She soaked up everything. He enjoyed watching her explore her new world.

"This village is so...so...quaint...no that's not the word I want." Nina grabbed the stick with some sort of food on it that Demos handed her. "What is this?"

"It is meat from the Trof, it is very good."

"Okay if you say so." Nina took a small bite, it tasted just like pork. "Barbarian barbeque," she chuckled. She saw the strange look on Demos' face. "It's a joke."

She continued to follow him around enjoying the sights, smells and sounds of the village. She noticed that there were two small suns instead of just one large one. "Beautiful," she exclaimed as the suns seemed to paint the sky a violet color.

Demos reached down and grabbed her hand as they headed for a stable. "This is Bella." He petted the dragon-looking creature gently on its snout.

"So this is a conja." Nina slowly extended her hand to pet the beast.

"You are not afraid of her?" He looked at Nina as she touched Bella with child like enthusiasm.

"Not at all, she didn't bite your hand off so what do I have to worry about." Nina petted Bella. The roughness of her scales felt strangely pleasant.

"Just remember wild conjas are very deadly and you should never approach one."

"Don't worry I will remember. I always liked dragons and Bella here is close enough to one."

"Demos!" A large warrior ran inside the stables.

"What's wrong?"

"A female escaped from the Larmat clan, but she is badly injured."

"Where is she?"

"Follow me."

Demos grabbed Nina's hand and followed the warrior to the Trial arena. "I didn't know what to do," the warrior said as they approached a black conja that had a dark-haired female lying next to it. "She must have stolen this conja to escape, though I don't recognize this female."

Demos went over to the female and gently rolled her over. She looked to have been beaten and raped. He didn't recognize her either. She must be from one of the other villages. He scooped her up in his arms. "Take care of the conja," he instructed the warrior. "Nina follow me."

"Is she going to be alright?"

"Tomar will know what to do, if not Kelila will."

Nina followed Demos back to the leader hut. She was briefly startled by Tomar's appearance until she saw the gentle way he examined the woman.

"Demos please go find Kelila. I want her here when the female wakes up. My presence alone may frighten her. You may leave your female here. I can guarantee she will be quite safe."

"I will be right back Nina." Demos hurried from the room.

"Your name is Nina, very pretty. I know the barbarians go by no last name, but you earthlings do, what is yours?"

"Ummm, Harris."

"Nina Harris, I like how that sounds. I am Tomar, like the barbarians we have no need for last names."

"Nice to meet you Tomar."

"Likewise, Nina."

"So, Demos has no last name?"

"No, but if he wished to be formal he would say something like I am Demos of the Dascon clan, son of Ranor."

"Aren't you the leader of the…"

"Rundal. Yes I am their leader."

"Then why are you here? I mean shouldn't you be with your people?"

"I am here to help Niro's mate birth her offspring. It is my pleasure to aid her."

"Tomar, will she be alright?" An older woman hurried into the room.

Nina noticed she had the same eyes Niro did. "Kelila is Niro's mother," Demos whispered into Nina's ear.

"Demos you will have to introduce me to your female." Kelila smiled at Nina.

"This is Nina," Demos said proudly.

"Hello Nina. I am Kelila mate of Hakan."

"Nice to meet you." Nina smiled at her. Kelila had a way about her that put anyone instantly at ease.

"How is Hakan?" Demos asked.

"He is stronger today." Kelila quickly went back to helping Tomar with the injured female.

Nina watched as both of them cleaned and tended to the female's injuries. She was lucky to have escaped.

"Where am I?" The female slowly sat up.

"You mustn't move too much," Kelila said. "You are safe now. You are in the main Dascon village."

"Niro…" Her voice was dry.

"Yes, I will take you to him as soon as you have rested. What is your name?"

"I am Safon from the village of Tanton."

"Why did you not just go back to your village? It is much closer to the Larmat lands," Demos asked.

"I have never flown a conja before. I am grateful it found its way here." Safon lay back down.

"Demos, you should send a scout to her village to let them know she is okay."

"Demos…" Safon turned her head and looked at the large, intimidating looking warrior. Her eyes fixated on the scar that went over his eye. Rasmus had done that to him, she kept thinking.

"What is it female?"

"You won the Trials. It is an honor to be in your presence."

"I think she should go rest somewhere." Nina couldn't stop herself from saying. She didn't like the way this woman was staring at Demos.

"Demos please carry Safon to my chambers," Kelila said.

Nina almost growled when Safon laid her head against Demos' chest as he carried her out of the room.

Tomar gently grabbed Nina's arm. "Jealousy lets you know what your heart really thinks." He smiled at her.

"That obvious huh?" Nina started to feel embarrass.

"I am afraid so. Now go before Demos finds you missing."

Nina hurried and caught up with Demos. The sooner that woman was out of his arms the better. Nina felt like kicking herself in the ass for feeling like this.

"Sit her down here. Thank you Demos." Kelila grabbed some extra furs.

Nina watched as Safon grabbed some of Demos' hair and smelled the fragrance of it. Her other hand slowly traveled down his well-muscled arm. "You are such a well built warrior," she cooed.

Nina's blood started to boil. For a woman who escaped sheer hell, this Safon sure seemed to recover quickly enough. One thing she knew for sure that bitch better just keep her hands off Nina's man…her heart started to pound in her chest. Demos was her man, damn it, yes she liked how that sounded.

"What is wrong, Nina?" Demos lightly stroked her cheek.

"Nothing," she said quickly.

He knew something was wrong with her, but he wouldn't press the issue right now.

"Can we go now?" Nina asked.

Demos grabbed her hand and led her to Niro's meeting chamber. Demos told one of the guards to go find Niro for him. "Tell me what is wrong?"

"What is wrong? Ha!" Nina paced back and forth.

"I don't understand your anger."

She glared up at him. "That Safon didn't seem that injured to me. She sure had the energy to flirt with you didn't she. I didn't see you telling her to knock it off." Her blood started to boil when she heard him start to laugh. "What in the hell is so funny?!"

"My little flower is jealous. I am very flattered." Demos grimaced when he felt her kick him hard in the stomach. "Ouch, that almost hurt." He continued to playfully chuckle.

"Almost hurt…well let's see how you like this." Nina jumped up and tried to land a front kick, but he moved out of the way.

"Missed me."

She did a series of kicks and punches but he dodged and blocked everyone. "Stay still damn it."

She punched and kicked until she finally landed a kick to his leg. He fell to the ground and just lay there.

"Demos…" She rolled him over and gasped when he grabbed her. He was laughing hard now.

"My flower likes to play rough. Later I will play rough with you, however Niro should be arriving soon." He quickly came back up to his feet with her in his arms. This impressed the hell out of her. His agility and strength was amazing.

"Demos?" Niro slowly walked into the room.

"Niro." Demos quickly put Nina down then gave her a playful pat on the ass. "A female named Safon has escaped from the Larmat. Your mother is tending to her now."

"Is she okay?"

"Yeah, I think she will be just fine," Nina injected.

Niro looked at Nina with a puzzled look. "Demos you will explain to me later."

"Your mother requested a scout to go to the female's village of Tanton."

"Alright, you pick which warrior to send."

Demos could see Niro was worried about something. "Is it alright for Nina to visit with Robin?"

"Yes, she is in the other chamber." Niro waited for Nina to leave. "Demos, a Larmat spy has been dispatched. One of our spies had reported in today."

"I will hunt down this spy."

"No, no one is allowed into the leader hut until the spy is found. I need you and all the warriors who are in the hut now to stay here. This female who was found where is she now?"

"Your mother's chamber."

"Keep an eye out, this Larmat warrior shouldn't be too hard to spot. But I want all the weaker males accounted for. Any new ones bring them to me."

"You think the spy is a weaker male?"

"It could be. A weaker male would have an easier time blending in. Now I must go check on this female Safon. I will find out who abducted her. Go find a reliable scout to notify her village."

"Yes Niro."

"Don't worry, your female will be alright. I will be posting two warriors at this door and the door to my chambers at all times." Niro was more than agitated. A spy, or worse an assassin was here somewhere waiting for the opportunity to hurt Robin and his son. Rai was becoming more and more unreliable. This female who had been lucky enough to escape the Larmat, he would have to allow her to stay until her village was notified. But most of all, his mind was on Robin, how much more could her little body take. The baby was causing her such discomfort and Niro was beyond afraid that Robin wouldn't survive giving birth. All these thoughts swirled in his mind as he went to check on Safon.

Chapter 8

Nina brushed Robin's long brown hair and then braided it up for her. Robin looked so uncomfortable, Nina wanted to do anything to help her out. Robin has been so nice to her since she came to Malka.

"Demos is officially your protector?"

"Yeah, I guess you can say that."

"Has anyone challenged him for you yet?"

"Challenged him?"

"Like what he did to Rai, challenged him to be your protector."

"No, nobody has threatened to kick his butt. Why?"

"I was just curious." Robin tried to get comfortable but found it almost impossible.

"Do you ever get jealous...you know when other women look at Niro?" Nina put a pillow behind Robin trying to help her get comfortable.

"Well, I didn't use to, but since Niro has become leader and I look like a beach ball, I have to admit I do get jealous every now and then, especially of the few females who don't have protectors yet."

"I thought all women have some sort of protector."

"Not if she isn't of age yet or her protector got killed in battle. Sometimes other Dascon villages give Niro females, which of course I don't like at all."

"What does he do with them?"

"He places them in a secured part of the leader hut until protectors are named for them."

"Hello Robin and Nina," Jamie said as she entered the chamber.

"Where have you been hiding?" Nina asked.

"Samson's chamber." She blushed. "Robin, you said you were going to explain the joining ceremony."

"Oh good, you are both here so I can tell you at the same time. Jamie has agreed to be Samson's mate so they will begin the joining ceremony. Basically she has agreed to marry him."

"Already, damn Jamie you don't waste time." Nina chuckled.

"Why wait, I know I love Samson. He has been very good to me."

"Jamie, for the next two weeks any male who wishes to challenge Samson for you will have to do so. Once you are joined with him, any male who dares to hurt you, Samson has the right to kill. Kelila said to me when I first was going through this that the more males that challenge Samson, the more honored you will be. I think it's stupid, but it's their tradition. Jamie, in these two weeks you must prove to Samson that you can satisfy his male needs, if you know what I mean. The night before the joining there will be a feast where you have to perform the dance of seduction."

"What?!" Jamie gasped.

"You have to seduce every male in the room with just your dance. Then when Samson thinks the frenzy has reached its peak, he will start to dance for you until he seduces you to take him right there in front of all the other males. Once he takes you, he must spill his seed onto a sacred platter. There will be ten other males in the room and each of them will take turns pleasuring you, and you have to pleasure them until they too spill their seed onto this platter. After this, each one presents you with something to show their respect for you."

"Excuse me?!" Nina gasped. "There is no way I am doing that and no offense Jamie, but I can't see you doing that either. I mean what in the hell do they do with the cum they collect on the damn platter anyways?"

"It goes to feed the flowers you will be carrying in the joining ceremony. Nina, did you ask Demos to be your mate?" Robin seemed excited.

"No, I am just getting to know the guy."

"Oh…" Robin looked disappointed. "Jamie just remember, once you are joined, it is forever. If you are caught cheating on Samson or he gets caught cheating on you, then you or him can be killed."

"Samson told me this. I know I am ready to be with him forever. I can't wait to have his baby."

"You will be able to once he drinks the sacred juice. But I will explain more about this when it's time for your joining ceremony."

"This is too much," Nina said, sitting back in her chair. "And what if a couple didn't want to go through all of that. What if they didn't want to get married, or joined as it is put here? Then what?"

"I really don't know Nina. You would have to ask Kelila."

Robin looked over to Nina. She could almost see the myriad of thoughts that were filling Nina's mind. "You know Nina you can talk to me about anything. Not all men are assholes."

"A good ninety percent of them are, though."

"You have been hurt a lot haven't you?"

"Yeah, so, what does that have to do with anything? You know I really don't want to talk about it okay? I don't mean to sound like a bitch but…"

"I understand."

"Anyways, Jamie here has to get prepared for her joining." Nina smiled. "Does she at least get to wear some sort of wedding gown for the actual ceremony?"

"Oh yes."

"Cool, okay Jamie let's discuss what you are going to wear."

ຂດຂດຂດ

Niro entered the chamber where Safon was being guarded. Niro nodded his head at the large warrior who was guarding the door.

"Who are you?" Safon climbed out of the bed and started to back away from Niro.

"I am Niro."

"Oh forgive me, great Niro." Safon came down to her knees in front of him.

"That is not necessary." Niro looked at her strange. This is how females greeted a Larmat leader.

"But…Rasmus told me this is what a female was required to do when in a leader's presence."

"It is not required by me. Please sit down. Don't fear me I will not harm you or rape you, nor will any other of my warriors."

Safon sat down on the bed and looked to the floor. Her body was still sore from what those two Larmat warriors had done to her. But it was worth it to be able to help Rasmus. She slowly looked up at Niro. He was even more handsome than rumors had stated and judging by his powerful body, she was sure he was every bit the skilled warrior too.

"When were you abducted?"

"Just a few weeks ago."

"This would explain your fresh bruises. Tomar said you will be alright and still able to carry children."

"That is a relief to hear."

"I am sending a scout to your village to inform them you are safe. Did you have a mate?"

"Yes, but he was killed trying to rescue me." Safon heard how Dascon males risked everything to save their mates.

"I am sorry to hear of your loss."

"How long before my village is notified? I am eager to go home."

"It will take at least a week for my scout to return. In the meantime you will stay in this chamber and not go outside of it without a guardian. I will not force you to choose a protector since you are grieving for your lost mate."

"Thank you great Niro." She bowed her head respectfully then watched him leave the room. She had one week to kill Robin and the baby. Once that scout got back Niro would learn of her lies.

She caught a glimpse of herself in the mirror and she cringed. She wanted her golden hair back, she hated looking like a Dascon female. Most of all she wanted back into Rasmus' arms. She closed her eyes and fell back into bed. But first she must find a way to get near Robin.

Chapter 9

Despite Robin's protest Nina walked back to Demos' chamber alone. She was mulling over everything Robin said about the joining ceremony. What a strange world Malka was. Nina reached Demos' chamber. She knew it was his because it had that same symbol his bracelet had. As she opened the door and prepared to enter she felt a strong hand on her arm. She quickly looked up and saw Demos, and she let out a sigh of relief.

"I have told you not to go anywhere without me. You could have gotten hurt," he growled.

"Calm down, nothing happened to me."

"But it could have. You must listen to me female."

"And you might just want to take a chill pill and let me go, damn it."

Demos dragged her into the chamber and slammed the door shut. He sat down on the bed and threw her over his knee. "You are to never go anywhere without me." He began to spank her hard across the ass.

"What in the hell do you think you are doing?!" She struggled to free herself.

"Giving you the spanking you so disparately need." He reached down and pulled her skirt up exposing her nicely rounded ass. He spanked her hard enough to paint her ass red.

"You bastard how dare you spank me like some child. Let me go now!"

"Not until you have learned to listen to your protector."

"Fuck you," she hissed at him.

He stood up and threw her on the bed. Before she had time to react he climbed on top of her. He pinned her arms above her head then held her with one arm. With the other he tore a piece of fabric from her dress. He used the fabric to tie her hands together.

"Let me up you bastard!"

"No," he growled as he tore her dress from her body. He forced her legs open and quickly removed his covering.

Nina wrapped her legs around him and mustering all the strength she had, she flipped him over so that now she was on top. He quickly rolled her over and pinned her under him again. He was breathing hard as he rammed his cock deeply into her. He thrust wildly into her as he held her hands firmly above her head. He could feel her legs wrap around him squeezing him tightly.

"You will obey me female," he rumbled as he thrust harder.

"Obey?" she said breathily. She looked up into in his face the anger, oh the lust in his eyes combined.

"I am your male and you will obey me!" he growled as he pulled his cock out and flipped her over. He scooted her to the end of the bed and tore another strip of fabric from her discarded dress. He secured her bound hands to the bedpost. He forced her upper body down onto the mattress then lifted her hips and drove his cock deeply into her. It all happened so fast that Nina had little time to react. He grunted and growled as he rode her. To her surprised she loved this act of dominance by him. She moaned loudly when she felt him bite her on the shoulder. He continued to growl as he rode her faster and harder.

He came up to his knees so he could watch his cock piston into her pussy. "You are mine, Nina. Mine to cherish and protect, do you understand? Do you female?" He slapped her ass hard.

"Yes," she whispered.

"Then you must obey me." He leaned over and pulled her up a little so now his body was covering her as he continued to thrust deeply into her. "I…" Demos tried to remember the words Robin used when she spoke tenderly to Niro, to let him know in her own language that she cared deeply for him. "I…love you Nina," he whispered into her ear.

"Demos…" Nina closed her eyes. Her orgasm was so strong, his words repeated over and over in her mind. He loved her…how was that possible, they barely knew each other. Fear, pleasure, warmth, it all combined in her.

Demos held her close as he slowly thrust into her. He felt her pussy clamp down on his cock telling him she had taken her pleasure. He reached under her and stroked her clit gently. He wanted her to feel more pleasure, wanted her to climax with him. He waited holding off his own release until he heard her sweet moans, then he allowed himself release. He held her so tightly to him as they enjoyed the afterglow of pleasure.

"I will be a good protector, Nina. I will fill your days with pleasure, joy and love. I swear it." Demos laid them down gently on the mattress then he reached up and untied her hands. He pulled her close and held her tightly. "You warm my heart, Nina. These are my people's words of love."

"You warm my heart, Demos," she said softly. She did love the big oaf, she realized that now and this scared her to death. She had been hurt so many times over her lifetime, so many that she began to think that true love and all that crap was a lie. She closed her eyes and snuggled closer to him.

"Please don't let this be a lie too." She repeated to herself.

ഊഊഊ

Niro held his hand on Robin's belly. "Let me go get Tomar," he said as he looked at the pain that washed Robin's face.

"Niro, I just began to have contractions. It would be silly to call Tomar now."

"Please little one, let me call Tomar."

"Okay Niro." She hated seeing that distressed look in his eyes.

"Hey girl it's about time you had that baby," Sabrina said as she hurried into the room with Saa right behind her.

Niro nodded his head to Saa, relieved that he was here to protect Robin, and then Niro hurried from the room to find Tomar.

Demos spotted Niro rushing down the corridor as he left his chamber. "Nina, we must go."

"Okay." She hurried behind him as he rushed to catch up with Niro.

"What has happened?" Demos said as he approached Niro.

"Robin is giving birth. I must find Tomar."

"I will find him. You should be with Robin."

"Hurry Demos."

Demos looked behind him to make sure Nina was still with him. "Go with Niro, Nina."

"Okay." Nina didn't want to get in the way so she did as Demos asked. She followed Niro back to his chamber.

"Wait in here for Demos."

Nina watched Niro as he hurried to Robin's side. Robin was in so much pain, but she tried to hide it from Niro.

"Little one." Niro squeezed her hand. It killed him to see her suffer so. There was little he could do to ease her pain.

"Niro." Kelila hurried into the room. She carried a small leather bag in her hand.

"Mother."

"Oh don't look so worried my son, females have been having children since time began. Bringing life into this world is very painful." She sat down next to Robin. "But the pain is soon forgotten." She reached into her bag and pulled out a small vile. "Drink Robin, this will ease your pain a bit." She placed the vile up to Robin's lips and tilted the bottle up. "There, that will help. Niro get a washbasin and a washcloth. You can wipe the sweat from her body."

Niro hurried and got the basin and cloth. He gently ran the cloth over Robin's face and chest.

"She is finally ready," Tomar said as he entered the room with Demos right behind him.

"Nina come over here and let's give Tomar a hand," Sabrina said.

Nina didn't realize she had a strong hold on Demos' hand until he brought her hand up and kissed it gently. "Go my flower I will be right here." Nina looked up into his eyes, the warmth in them was foreign to her, until he came into her life, she had never seen someone look at her this way. She smiled at him then went over to Sabrina.

"Okay, what do you want me to do?" Nina asked.

"Hold her other hand," Tomar said gently.

"Nina, I warn you I am going to squeeze the heck out of your hand. Ask Niro?" Robin squeezed both Niro and Nina's hand tightly.

"Little one." Niro kissed her on the forehead while he looked over to Tomar. He was talking to Kelila and Niro didn't like that look on his mother's face.

"Niro you have to come with me." Kelila hurried over to him.

"Why?" Niro came up to his feet.

"I have to cut her belly open and remove the child," Tomar quickly said.

"I will not allow you to do such a thing to her!" Niro rumbled.

"Niro, calm down." Robin reached up for his arm.

"If I don't cut her belly and take the baby this way. She will die, Niro, and so will your son."

Nina looked at Niro. He had turned pale as he sat back down.

"Niro, come on, let Tomar do what he must." Demos went to him.

"They do this kind of delivery all the time on Earth," Nina added.

"That's right Niro, I will be fine."

"I love you Robin." Niro kissed her then her belly. He allowed Demos to escort him out of the room. Saa remained to stand guard over the women.

"Robin, this will put you to sleep," Tomar said as he placed a strange looking mask on her face.

Nina watched as Robin quickly fell asleep. Tomar went to work. Nina couldn't take her eyes off of him, the speed and precision in which he worked. Kelila assisted him while Sabrina made ready the basinet for the baby. Nina watched in amazement as Tomar pulled the large baby from Robin's body. Within seconds the infant began to wail. Nina smiled and held Robin's hand tightly. Tomar handed the baby to Kelila then went to work sewing Robin back up.

"Is she going to be alright?" Nina asked as Tomar sewed the last stitch and applied some sort of ointment to the wound.

"Yes, she should be just fine."

Nina jerked up when she heard the door burst open. Demos was trying to restrain Niro but finally gave up and let him enter.

"Robin?" Niro looked at Tomar.

"She will be just fine, Niro. Why don't you say hello to your new son."

Niro slowly walked over to the basinet where Sabrina and Kelila were finishing cleaning the baby up.

"He looks just like you did when you were a baby," Kelila said, picking the baby up and handing him over to Niro.

Niro gently took the baby in his arms. He smiled looking down into the baby's sweet face.

"Niro bring our son over to me," Robin said groggily.

Nina stood up and went over to Demos. He wrapped his arm around her and pulled her close to his side.

"What is your son's name, Niro?" Demos asked.

Niro looked to Robin. "Well what is his name?" Robin smiled at him.

"Zenos," Niro proudly exclaimed. "It means one with great strength." He looked to Robin for her approval.

"Zenos, I like it." She smiled up at Niro as he carefully placed Zenos in her arms.

Saa and Demos cried out a battle cry that startled Nina. Soon Niro joined them. It was an odd picture, three large barbarians letting out these fierce cries. And yet, little Zenos wasn't afraid, as if he knew the three men were only celebrating.

Kelila hurried to Robin's side. Nina thought Kelila already looked like the proud grandmother. "We must show your father his new grandson," Kelila said as she rubbed the baby's cheek. "And you must show the people, Niro."

Nina looked to Demos, not quite sure what they were supposed to do now.

"Demos, please stay with Robin," Niro said as he gently took the baby back into his arms.

"Yes Niro."

"Thank you Tomar," Niro said, before he left the room with Kelila, Saa and Sabrina following him.

"Your baby is beautiful," Nina said.

"He is, isn't he." Robin smiled.

Nina was startled again when she heard the sound of many male warriors crying out fierce battle cries.

"Niro has announced to the people Zenos' arrival." Robin smiled over to Nina. "I wish I could be there when he shows Zenos to his grandfather Hakan."

"No, Robin, I am afraid you will have to lie in bed for a few days," Tomar said.

"Will I be able to come to the Rundal's life ceremony?"

"Yes, you should be strong enough then. Now you should rest." Tomar handed her a small vile. "This will help you sleep."

"Thank you Tomar," Robin said sleepily. Soon she was fast asleep.

Demos nodded his head respectfully to Tomar as he left the room. "Come Nina, let's let Robin sleep. I will stand guard outside her room."

Nina followed Demos out of the room, then she sat down on the floor next to him. "That baby was cute, but very big. Damn he was the size of a six month old on Earth."

"This is the normal size of Malka infants."

Nina looked up Demos' leg. His legs were strong and well-muscled and from her vantage point, she could see up his loincloth. "How long will Niro and the others be gone?"

"For awhile, he must show Zenos to the people, then I am sure Hakan would like to spend time with him. Why?"

"Nothing really." Nina let her hand move up his thigh until she cupped his balls in her hand. His cock began to become hard. "Mmm, spread your legs a little wider for me," she purred. He did what she asked. Nina kissed up his leg, she moved the fabric aside a little and let her tongue lick the exposed part of his balls.

Demos didn't care if someone saw them. He quickly removed his covering, giving her full access to him. "Nina…" he sighed as she licked up the length of his cock. He groaned when she took the head into her mouth. He looked down at her kneeling there in front of him with her mouth full of his cock. He gently cupped her head pushing down a little. "Take all of my cock down your throat, please Nina."

"Ah, since you put it that way, baby, mmmm."

Demos growled as he watched his huge cock disappear into her mouth. She slid her mouth up and down on his cock. Her moans vibrated on his cock adding a new sensation, almost driving him mad. He didn't want to come yet, oh no, not yet.

"Come on, fuck my mouth," Nina growled.

Demos grabbed her head then started thrusting his cock deeper and faster into her mouth. "You like that?" He smiled down at her. "Do you?" Her moans made him thrust harder. He felt her nails dig into his thigh as he drove his cock harder and harder. "I am going to take my pleasure. Oh damn it I can't hold it back."

80

"Fuck my mouth, come down my throat," she moaned as she slapped him hard on the ass.

"Oh, yesss…" He grabbed her head and fucked her face, faster and harder. He pushed his whole cock into her mouth and held her there as he shot his cum down her throat. He grinded her head against him as his body shuddered. He slowly pulled his cock out of her mouth then lifted her up into his arms.

"My turn," he growled as he pinned her against the wall, lifting her up until her legs rested on his shoulders. He pulled her covering off with one tug.

"Oh shit!" she exclaimed as he licked hungrily at her pussy. She reached down and grabbed his head trying to steady herself. He was standing straight up with his face buried in her pussy as he pinned her to the wall. God, she wished she could have filmed this.

"Bury my face in your pussy," he said as he flicked his tongue over her clit.

Nina grabbed his head firmly and pushed his face hard into her pussy. She rubbed his face in her pussy as he licked and sucked at her. His muffled moans were driving her crazy. He reached up and squeezed her ass hard as he continued to wallow his face in her pussy.

"Demos!!" she cried out as the first orgasm filled her, but still he ate her pussy. "Somebody is going to come," she said breathily.

"Yeah, you, now fuck my face." He stuck his tongue deep in her. She moved her hips back and forth feeling his tongue go in and out of her.

"Oh Demos." She held him firmly to her as she came again. "Fuck me, please fuck me."

Demos shrugged his shoulders hard knocking her legs from him then he pinned her again against the wall, this time his cock filled her pussy.

"Yes Demos, harder, harder!!" She dug her nails into his back.

He rammed his cock into her over and over. "Damn female, I am going to come already."

"Oh baby you deserve it, let me hear you come."

Her whole body trembled when he cried out his orgasm. She held him tightly to her as she felt his cock pulse deeply inside her.

"I see you two are getting along well," Sabrina chuckled.

"Oh shit." Nina held Demos to her to cover her body.

"Damn, you two made me horny as hell," Saa rumbled.

"Let's let them get dress. You may want to hurry. Niro is coming back here."

Demos and Nina quickly got dressed. Nina was so embarrassed but Demos didn't seem bothered by them being caught at all.

"That was so good, Nina," Demos purred into her ear.

"Damn straight it was, wasn't it." Nina could feel her desire for him starting to build just thinking about what they just did.

"When we get back to our chamber later, I am going to eat your pussy for an hour." He licked at her earlobe.

"Stop that now before I fuck you right here." Nina pushed him away.

"That is suppose to make me want to stop, mmm, I would love for you to fuck me right here."

"Behave yourself. Here comes Niro and little Zenos."

"Alright, I will be good for now." Demos gave her a playful swat on the ass as they followed Niro back into the chamber.

Chapter 10

Rai gripped Safon's hips tighter as she rode his cock. He watched her breasts bounce up and down as he lay there. Oh, her pussy felt so good as it milked his cock, trying to coax his nectar out. Niro had forbidden any warrior to take Safon, but Rai didn't care. The female had offered her sweet pussy to him, so the hell with Niro.

"Oh you are magnificent," Safon purred as she rode him faster. She kept her eyes closed wanting to imagine that it was Rasmus' cock she was enjoying.

Rai grabbed her hips and slammed her down onto his cock, over and over as his pleasure built and built. "That's it female squeeze your pussy, oh yes…mmmm," he moaned, removing his hands from her hips allowing her to send him over the edge.

Safon smiled as he cried out with pleasure. She needed this warrior to get closer to Niro and she was willing to pleasure him to accomplish this. She felt him toss her to the side. She quickly sat up and covered herself.

"How many of those Larmat warriors used that pussy of yours?" Rai asked as he put his covering back on.

"Too many."

"That's a shame, otherwise I would be your protector." Rai looked her over. "I don't want a female who was used by other warriors." He sat down on the bed next to her. "The hair on your pussy is a golden color, this is strange. I thought only Larmat sluts' pussies were covered with golden hair."

"My mate didn't care what color my pussy hair was, why should you?"

"I don't care what color your pussy hair is, as long as that pussy is always ready for me."

"When can I see Niro?"

"Why?"

"I want to know more about our leader. You are one of his finest warriors aren't you?"

"Damn right I am. I will take you to Niro this afternoon. Keep your ass in this room until I escort you back." He stood up and looked down at her. "Mmm, but first…" He removed his covering and held his hard cock in his hand. "Come over here and suck my cock."

Safon put on a smile, though she felt disgusted having to service this Dascon warrior. She took his cock into her mouth and began to suck. She felt him grip her head as his cock thrust into her mouth. His grunts and moans made her angry. But anything was worth it for Rasmus.

ఐఐఐ

Rai almost growled at Demos as he and Safon approached the meeting room. "Where is your female?" he hissed at Demos.

"Nina is none of your concern." Demos looked down at Safon.

"This female is none of your concern Demos. She wants to see Niro, so move out of the way."

Safon stepped back a little, she could feel the tension in the air between the two. She was sure a fight would break out at any moment. She was genuinely surprised when Demos stepped aside. She followed Rai into the chamber.

"What is it Rai?" Niro was with a group of weaker males. They all seemed to huddle in a corner as if they were terrified of Niro.

"This female wants to spend time with you."

Niro turned and looked down at Safon. "Sit over there." He pointed to a chair off to the side. "You may go Rai."

"I can help you do whatever is you are doing." Rai smiled seeing the terror in the weaker males' faces. He recognized some of them. Oh yeah his cock knew several of those mouths.

"Tell Demos to come inside. You may stay as well if you wish." Niro turned back toward the weaker males.

Demos entered the chamber and stood off to the side. He looked at the twenty or so weaker males. He couldn't understand their fear. Demos feared no man.

"Do you recognize any of them?" Niro asked as he slowly pulled his sword from its sheath, causing the herd of weaker males to back up.

"The two in the back work at the market," Demos said.

Niro dismissed the two.

"A lot of them are just bitches, who are housed in the whorehouse," Rai added.

"Is this true?" Niro turned to Demos.

"I wouldn't know I don't use weaker males."

Niro turned back toward the weaker males. He had never used one of them either. "Rai, who handles the males that live in the weaker males' hut?"

"I will go round him up for you." Rai left the room and soon returned with an older warrior.

"I am Taji, great Niro." He bowed his head at Niro.

"Are these…" Niro didn't really know what to call them.

"Bitches, are they your bitches Taji?" Rai injected.

Taji walked over to them and looked them over. "Yes, Niro these are my weaker males."

"Why is it I have never seen any of them around?" Niro asked.

"They never leave the hut, Niro. They are too busy servicing your warriors."

"That is awful!" Robin exclaimed as she entered the room.

"Little one, you should be resting." Niro went over to her and gently kissed her.

"Your mother took Zenos to visit your father and I thought I would come and spend some time with you. But...Niro it isn't right to keep these males locked up like that."

"Weaker males...and their only purpose is to suck cock or get fuck like a woman would," Rai said.

"It is still wrong." Robin glared over to Rai. She didn't like this warrior at all. Most of Niro's prized warriors she admired, but Rai, oh no, he was an arrogant asshole. She could tell he cared little for her as well.

"Niro, you are not going to let your female interfere with how you rule are you?" Rai quickly turned when he heard Demos unsheathed his sword.

"You will not question Niro," Demos growled.

"Enough!" Niro held his sword tightly in his hand. "Rai, you may leave now."

"Your female makes you weak Niro," Rai almost growled.

"Are you challenging me Rai?" Niro placed Robin behind him.

"I wouldn't dream of doing so Niro. Forgive my words." Rai bowed his head then left the room.

"Do you want me to kill him Niro?" Demos asked.

"No, he is arrogant but he is a very skilled warrior. Besides..." Niro pulled Robin over to him. "Robin wouldn't want someone to die just because they spoke their mind." He smiled down at her.

"Thank you Niro." She nuzzled her head against his arm.

"As you wish." Demos sheathed his sword.

"Where is Nina?" Robin asked.

"She is spending time with Jamie." Demos smiled. He remembered the unbelievable blow job she gave him just before he escorted her to Jamie's chamber. He quickly thought of unpleasant things trying to keep his cock from getting hard.

Robin grabbed a plate of fruit and went over to the weaker males. They backed away from her. "Please don't be afraid. Niro, tell them that it is alright."

"Little one…" Niro saw that look on her face. She wanted so much to give these males a brief moment of peace. How could he possibly say no to her request? "Do not fear, I won't harm you for being so close to my female." Niro saw the weaker males visibly relax as they took the fruit from Robin.

"Niro, I must go train if you are no longer in need of me."

"Oh, go train Demos." Niro walked over to Safon. "What is it that you wish to talk to me about?"

"I just want to watch you for a little while. I want to tell the people in my village all about you. Your mate is a very kind female."

"Yes she is."

"I wouldn't mind spending some time with her, of course with your permission first."

"Little one, would you like to spend some time with Safon?"

"That would be lovely. We can go see what Jamie and Nina are up to. Would you like that Safon?"

"Very much so."

"I will escort you to Jamie's chamber," Niro said. "Taji, take your males back to your hut."

"Yes Niro. Come on bitches, let's move," Taji growled.

"Don't call them that!" Robin snapped.

Taji looked over to Niro. "Don't call them that in her presence Taji."

"Yes Niro."

"Come Safon, let's go see what the others are up too." Robin wrapped her arms around one of Niro's arms as he led them to Jamie's chamber. Safon was pleased, she will be able to gain Robin's trust now, then she smiled as she followed them down the corridor.

ಐಐಐ

Robin gave Niro a kiss and watched him post another warrior by the door. Samson was already there and welcomed the company of the other warrior.

"Hey guys, this is Safon," Robin said as she entered the room.

"Hello Safon, Jamie is busy picking out her joining dress. Robin you are looking a lot better today," Nina said. She would try to be civil to this woman, even though she didn't like her all that much.

"The medicine Tomar gave me is wonderful. I am still a little sore but that is it."

"Where is Zenos?" Jamie asked.

"He is with his grandparents."

Safon listened to the women prattle on. She couldn't risk killing Robin now, besides Zenos wasn't with her. It would be easier to kill them both at the same time. She never heard of a joining ceremony before. Only the strongest of Larmat warriors were permitted to have females and the higher ranking he was, the more females he could have. She knew she would have to share Rasmus with several other females. It totally baffled her that Niro had only one mate. Though listening to these women talk she grew envious.

"Samson has fought off like six warriors already. Is that good?" Jamie asked.

"Yes, it is," Robin replied.

"All this macho crap is starting to get on my nerves," Nina sighed.

"I think it's sweet that Samson wants to protect me. I kind of like him escorting me around, and I have to admit I kind of enjoy when he growls at any other man that gets near me. It's so…animalistic." Jamie beamed.

"It's so irritating. I am sorry Jamie but I like walking around by myself. I sure the hell don't like Demos telling me what to do all the time."

"Tell me Nina, did Demos tell you to visit Jamie?" Robin asked.

"Well no, I told him I wanted to talk with her."

"Hmmm, Niro gives me anything I want. The only thing he asks of me is that I let him protect me. And what I have seen so far between you and Demos, it's pretty much the same way."

"Yeah, sort of…but I don't like having to have someone always there with me."

"I will live with this small thing, besides I like Samson to be around me all the time, or knowing that he has placed me in the care of another warrior he trust when he has to train or do something where I can't go with him."

"Well I am glad you two have resigned yourself to being a well guarded treasure. But I want to get out there and explore. Come on, we are on a different freaking planet."

"And I am sure Demos would love to show you everything," Robin added.

Safon was half paying attention to them now. She needed to get into Robin's chambers and somehow get her and Zenos alone, and she had less than a week to do it. "I would give anything to be in my mate's arms again," Safon quietly said. She felt Robin grab her hand. She would use Robin's sympathy to gain Niro's trust. Yes, this was perfect. Safon was pleased with herself as she faked a few tears and allowed Robin to hold her.

ಋಋಋ

Nina left Jamie's chamber shortly after Robin and Safon did. She didn't have a guard or anything, for once she wanted to walk around and explore a little on her own. She knew Demos would probably have a cow about it, but she would deal with it later.

She headed outside and through the gardens. The vibrant colors of the flowers were breathtaking. When she went to ask the weaker male about the flowers he fled in terror. Nina tried to tell him it was alright, the only thing the male said as he ran away was that he feared Demos.

Nina was drawn over to the training grounds when she heard the sound of swords clashing. But before she got there she was grabbed from behind.

"I want some of your pussy, female," a deep masculine voice growled.

"Let me go asshole." Nina kicked him as hard as she could. He let her go and she quickly turned to face her attacker. Her heart hammered into her chest. This guy was a big dude, just like the rest of these damn warriors.

"You will pay for that female."

"Come on, bring it on big boy." Nina jumped out of the way when he lunged at her. She could see the confusion in his face. She used this to her advantage delivering kick after kick, until finally the large warrior backed up a little.

"Demos deserves better than you," he said as he wiped the blood from his nose. "No warrior will challenge him for the likes of you. Huh, you might as well be a male. You don't act like a delicate female." He turned and walked away from her.

Nina sank down to the ground trying to catch her breath. The mixture of fear and exertion had drained her. "I act like a male, why, because I can defend myself?" Nina was more than a little angry at his words. She then remembered what Robin said about warriors challenging a protector, the more they challenge the protector, the more honor is brought to his female and him. And so far that fatheaded barbarian was right; no one had challenged Demos for her. She wondered if this bothered Demos.

She slowly got up and continued to the training grounds. Her breath caught when she saw Demos. He was training with three other warriors. She moved slowly toward them, but made sure to keep a safe distance from them. Demos moved with such speed and skill that he easily overpowered his three attackers. The clanking of their swords rang out as they battled. Demos' body dripped with sweat as he fought on. Nina couldn't take her eyes off of him. He was magnificent, the way his body moved, and the fierce look in his eyes, everything about him was amazing. She tore her gaze away long enough to see a large group of younger warriors had gathered to watch Demos trained. Pride swelled in her watching the look of admiration on the young warriors' faces. She looked back at Demos and watched as he won his match. She smiled hearing the howls and cheers coming from the other warriors. Demos simply helped his opponents back up and told them good fight. He didn't pose or howl, hell she half-assed expected him to beat at his chest, but he did none of these things. He just wiped the sweat from his face and drank down some water then sheathed his sword.

She watched one of the younger warriors walk over to Demos then point at her. Oh, oh, she was busted. She saw the anger flash in his eyes as their gaze met. Demos headed straight for her.

"What in the hell are you doing out here and where is your escort?"

"I wanted to look around by myself for a little while."

"How many times have I told you that this is dangerous? Are you hurt, did anyone attack you?"

"This one idiot tried but…"

"Who?!"

"I don't know who he was. Hey I took care of it, so calm down."

Demos grabbed her and looked her over for injuries. "Did he mount you?"

"Mount me? No, he didn't mount me. What a crude way to put that!"

"Damn it Nina!" Demos' voice boomed.

"You were amazing out there."

"What?"

"You fought off three of those big guys. Wow! I would love to be able to use a sword like that." Nina smiled looking out over the training grounds again.

"My flower," Demos put his hand gently under her chin and tilted her head so she was looking right into his eyes, "please don't walk around by yourself again."

"I will try."

"No, you will do."

"Oh come on Demos. I am not exactly helpless." She was surprised when he grabbed her by the hand and led her out into the training field. He scooped up one of the training swords and gave it to her.

"Oh man this thing is heavy."

"Attack me."

"I might hurt you."

"Just do it."

Nina lifted the sword and charged at him. The sword was very heavy so her swings were very easy for Demos to avoid, then he swung his sword and knocked hers right out of her hands.

"Okay, what are you trying to prove here?"

"You are not trained to defend yourself against a sword. You couldn't even block one of my attacks and I used only a small portion of my strength."

"I can use my karate to defend myself."

"This is true, but what will you do when a warrior draws his sword?"

"I don't think that will happen."

"It does happen Nina. Some warriors have drawn their sword and killed females and weaker males out of anger. The warrior you fought off…what would have happened if you angered him enough that he drew his sword?"

"Then teach me to use a sword." She looked up at him.

"Nina…" Demos gently caressed her cheek. "If you promise not to wander around alone I will teach you to use a sword." He couldn't help but smile seeing her face light up. Yes, this is what she wanted. To hell with the rest of the warriors, let them talk, he was going to train his beautiful flower to be a skilled warrior.

"I promise, when do we start?" she said excitedly.

"As soon as I have the weapon maker create a sword that you can wield."

"Thank you Demos." She wrapped her arms around him and hugged him tightly.

Demos stroked her hair. He heard what some of the warriors were saying and he knew that none of them would challenge him for her. But he didn't care. His female was unique and that is why he loved her so much. He hugged her tighter to him. He wanted so much to ask her to join with him, but he had to give her more time. He was willing to wait for her.

Chapter 11

Nina woke up in the morning snuggled against Demos. The warm light of the morning filled the room. She slowly sat up, her eyes lingered over Demos' strong chest. She looked around the room then smiled when she spotted the braided cloth cord of the curtains. She quietly climbed out of bed then pulled Demos knife from its sheath. She could picture how this knife looked strapped to his well muscled thigh. She hurried to the curtain and cut two lengths of cloth cord off. "This will work," she whispered. She headed back over to the bed. She put his knife back in its sheath then stood by the side of the bed. Damn, Demos was so beautifully male. She licked her lips, hungry to taste his glorious body. She pulled the furs down exposing the lower half of his body to her hungry gaze. She grabbed one of his arms and tried to lift it up to the bedpost.

"What are you doing, Nina?" he said sleepily.

"I want to play a game."

"Mmm, what kind of game?"

She smiled watching his cock harden. "It's called you are my prisoner." She placed his hand by the bedpost then tied his wrist up to it. She climbed over him and did the same for the other.

"You believe this rope will hold me, huh?" he playfully scoffed.

"I am going to have fun finding out." She removed her silk wrapping, loving the way his eyes feasted on her body. She started at his feet, she let her hands and mouth explore his flesh. She sucked on each toe loving the groans coming from him.

"I must warn you, Nina, it is unwise to tease a Dascon male for too long."

"Oh really, what will happen if I do?" She took his foot and rubbed it over her breasts. She then slowly started to lick and kiss up his leg.

"I will lose control."

"Uh, sounds yummy." Her tongue flicked over his balls before she took as much as she could of them into her mouth and lightly sucked.

"Oh damn it female," he groaned. "I will fuck that pussy until you are sore if I lose control." He pulled on the ropes a little.

"I will chance it." She smiled up at him as she licked at the head of his cock.

"Take my cock into your mouth and suck on it," he moaned.

"In due time." She kissed and licked at his stomach as she placed his huge cock between her breasts. She rubbed back and forth engulfing his cock in the tunnel her breasts made.

"Fuck me," he started to growl.

"Oh not yet." She moved up to his chest taking one of his nipples into her mouth while she rubbed her pussy up and down on his cock.

"Take me female, before I break these damn ropes and fuck the hell out of you." His voice was so deep and so full of lust, need and want. She moved up to his neck and bit softly. She licked at his earlobes.

"Nina," he growled.

She kissed his lips then stuck her tongue deeply into her mouth. He probed her mouth with his tongue. He groaned when she sucked on his tongue. She moved up covering his face with her breasts, but not allowing him to suckle. She arched up and ran her hands up his strong arms.

"Oh, I am going to have to start all over," she purred as she moved her body back down his.

"Fuck me now, female," he growled loudly.

"Patience warrior." She climbed off him. She let her hands wander down her own body, cupping her breast with one hand and letting the other head down to her pussy.

"No more," Demos boomed.

Nina gasped as he snapped the ropes. He grabbed her and threw her on the bed. Her head was facing the foot of the bed when he grabbed her hips and lifted her up as his cock rammed into her. He thrust hard and fast pushing her over the end of the bed. She reached her hands up and steadied herself. He rammed his cock over and over into her as she tried to balance herself. Her upper body was hanging completely off the bed.

"Demos," she moaned when he howled. She was surprised when he flipped her over and entered her again. His cock was already hard again pounding deep inside her, he reached down and pulled her up to him by her hair. His arm wrapped around her waist as he continued to drive himself into her. He bit her shoulder as he came again. He threw her on the bed then straddled her waist.

"Damn!" she exclaimed as she watched his cock get hard again.

"Suck my cock," he growled as he leaned over her. She eagerly took his cock into her mouth. The mental image of him lying on top of her, fucking her mouth excited her. She reached up and grabbed his ass urging him to go deeper into her mouth. She wanted to feel his cock down her throat. He thrust his cock deeper and deeper down her throat, growling and grunting as he felt her suck hard on him. He moaned hearing the sucking noise coming from her. He thrust harder and faster until he came. He thrust hard one final time keeping his cock buried to the hilt down her throat. His frenzy had been sated as he felt her still suckling on his cock He looked down and watched as he slowly pulled his cock out of her mouth.

"Did I hurt you?" he quietly said as he rolled over to the side of her.

"No, baby," she purred as she lowered herself down his body. "I want to try something else," she said, kissing his cock then sat next to him. "Get up on your knees and spread your legs open." She smiled seeing his cock harden. Damn did this man have stamina or what.

Demos groaned watching her lying under him. "Nina," he sighed, feeling her tongue on his balls.

"Dip your balls into my mouth over and over while I suck and lick at them."

"Oh yesss," he hissed as he did as she asked. Slowly he moved his hips up and down as she bathed his balls with her tongue. He loved the slight pulling when she sucked at them as he continued to move. He saw her hand go down to her pussy. He bent over and stuck his tongue into her pussy. He wrapped his arms around her hips and lifted her up. He spread his legs further apart and started to move his hips again. He bent over slightly and licked at her pussy. Nina wrapped her arms around his legs to steady herself. Luckily she was a flexible person or otherwise this strange position would hurt. He moved his tongue rapidly over her clit thoroughly enjoying the taste of her.

"Oh shit, right there Demos, oh yes, yes…fuck yes."

He buried his face in her pussy as she orgasm, moving his face back and forth wanting to be covered by her sweet nectar. He moved his hips back and forth and up and down, rubbing his balls on her face as she sucked and licked at him.

He lowered her down then grabbed his cock and positioned it by her mouth. "Suck me Nina." He leaned over and buried his face back in her pussy as he slowly thrust into her mouth.

"Nina…" He arched up as he came. He felt her smack his ass. He pulled his cock out and was surprised when she grabbed his hips and pulled him down on her. She buried her face in his balls inhaling his scent deeply, then she let his hips go. She kissed his balls one last time then moved out from under him. Before she knew what happened he pinned her under him and drove his cock into her again.

"Damn Demos, how many times can you get that cock of yours hard?"

"As many times as you wish me too."

He fucked her hard and fast from behind, gripping her hips tightly.

"Demos, bite me, pin me under you," she sighed.

"My female," he growled as he leaned over and bit her shoulder, pinning her under him.

"Growl Demos, oh please keep growling." She felt her orgasm build, when she heard his growls it made her whole body explode with pleasure. "Come on me, oh please come on me," she said breathily.

He pulled his cock out and arched back up. He stroked his cock a couple of times and then came all over her ass and back.

"Yes, Demos yes," she sighed, feeling his warm cum spray on her.

He collapsed on her making sure he wasn't crushing her. He held her tightly enjoying being so close to her.

"I am going to have to tie you up more often, holy crap…oh…that was so good," she cooed, snuggling closer to him.

"Mmmm," was all he replied.

ഞ‌ഞ‌ഞ

"You are what?!" Niro bellowed.

"I am going to teach Nina to fight with a sword," Demos replied.

"She will get hurt." Niro walked over to the balcony. What in the hell was Demos thinking?

"She is my concern Niro."

"No male will want to go to battle with her."

"I don't want her to go to battle. I just want her to be able to defend herself."

Niro turned to him. "Isn't that what you are for?"

"I would give my life to defend her. She needs this and I will give it to her."

"Demos I am sure you have heard what other warriors are saying about your female?"

"I have heard some of it. Of course no one will say these things to my face. Besides, what about your female? They talk of her, too."

"Watch your words, Demos," Niro growled.

"I am not saying anything about Robin. In fact I think she is a very kind and generous female. But others believe she will make you weak."

"I have heard them. She makes me think. She doesn't make me weak."

"Still you don't allow others to interfere with your relationship with your female. Why should I allow anyone to interfere with me and Nina's relationship? I am a loyal warrior, will always be one. Haven't I earned the right to live with my female any way I chose?"

"Go then, train her to use a sword, but you will not strike down any warrior who speaks ill of it."

"Thank you Niro."

Niro just nodded his head. He heard Demos leave the room. He looked out over the village. Did his people think he was weak?

"Niro?" Robin stood next to him. She had Zenos cradled in her arms.

"You will not question me again in front of any of my warriors."

"What?"

"You heard me female. Stay in this chamber until I return."

"What has gotten into you?"

"Do as I say." Niro started to walk away.

"Wait, what has happened?"

"I will not let my warriors think I am weak," he bellowed.

"Who says you are weak?"

"The males who have seen you question our ways and me giving into you."

Zenos started to fuss as if he could feel the tension between his parents. "Well I am sorry, Niro. I will remember not to speak my mind in front of your warriors. Take your son." She handed Zenos to Niro. "So, it's okay for me to speak openly, just as long as it's not in front of some male right?"

Niro walked over to Zenos' basinet and set him in it gently. He turned back to Robin. "I am leader of Dascon. I can't let my people think I am weak."

"You are not weak Niro. But you are making me very angry right now. So I am just going to leave and let you cool down, before we say things to hurt each other."

"You will stay in this chamber as I have commanded you to."

Robin just looked at him and started to leave. She was surprised when he grabbed her arm and pulled her to him. "You will stay in this chamber."

"Let me go."

"Obey me female," he bellowed.

Zenos started to cry and Robin hurried over to him. "I don't know what has gotten into you...but." She cradled Zenos in her arms. "I thought you valued my opinions, Niro. I thought I was free to express them, but apparently I was wrong."

Niro watched her trying to hold back her tears. "Little one...I am sorry," he said quietly as he sat down on the bed. "Demos is going to train Nina to use a sword. The other warriors will not like this..." Niro felt her hand on his back as she sat down next to him. "Some of my warriors think I am weak because I allow you to speak your mind." He looked at her, the tears that ran down her face tore at him. "I don't know what to do, little one."

"We will work it out." She nuzzled to him. He wrapped his arm around and pulled her and Zenos closer.

"I am sorry."

"Shh, I should of thought about how your warriors would see things. I will try not to say anything in front of them."

Niro was mad at himself for lashing out at her. So many things filled his mind. He lay back taking them with him. He laid Zenos on his chest and held Robin close to him as she snuggled by his side. He still hasn't found the spy, yet this weighed the heaviest on his mind. He could feel Robin and Zenos were in danger and yet he couldn't see where the danger would come from. He couldn't live without his family. Zenos cooed as he laid his head on Niro's chest, he began suckling on his thumb. Niro looked at his son, then Robin. He had to find this spy, this assassin, but he had no idea where to look. He had the whole hut searched, the village, the surrounding area, but no sign of a Larmat warrior. There were no new weaker males in the village. Niro closed his eyes and held Zenos and Robin close.

Chapter 12

"The festival of what?" Nina said as she walked beside Demos through the village.

"The Festival of Life. Since Tomar has stayed and taken care of Robin, Niro insisted we celebrate this Rundal holiday with Tomar."

"Ah, is it simply a festival because they are happy they are alive?"

"Well, I'm pretty sure the Rundals are happy to be alive, but no, it's the time when their eggs hatch."

"Eggs? Okay. You know I don't even want to picture that in my mind."

"A Rundal's offspring is quite cute."

"I am sure it is." Nina smiled up at him. She could see that he has wanted to ask her something all day and it must be very important for him to look so nervous. "How many Rundal are coming to the village?"

"About thirty, the others are staying in their village to celebrate."

Nina saw about a dozen warriors take to the sky on the backs of their conjas. "Where are they going?"

"They will protect the Rundal village during the celebration. With so many young being hatched it is too tempting a target for the Larmat Clan."

"This Larmat Clan sound like a bunch of assholes."

"They have no respect for life. Power seems to be the only thing they cherish."

"Demos, may I ask you something?" Nina said as he led her to an open field. He sat down and she sat next to him.

"You may ask me anything."

"How did you get this?" She ran her finger lovingly over the scar on his face.

"Rasmus' blade."

"Isn't he the assholes', I mean Larmat leader?"

"He is now. I was only sixteen when the Larmat attacked a small border village. It was my first real battle and I suspect Rasmus too. My father was with me in this battle and I wanted to make him proud. When Rasmus' blade cut my eye, I couldn't let it phase me, even though I couldn't see from this eye, I still can't." Demos touched his eye. "I would have killed him, but he ran from the battle. My father stopped me from pursuing him. He said it was cowardly to chase down a retreating enemy."

Nina saw Demos' proud smile. "Your father was proud of you wasn't he?"

"Yes, very proud."

She saw a sadness creep across his face. "What was your father's name?"

"Ranor. He was killed trying to rescue my mother from the Larmat warriors who kidnapped her."

"Oh, how awful. But I thought Larmat warriors had never reached the main village of Dascon."

"They haven't. My mother, her name was Jeneva, was aiding the people of the village who were just attacked. My father had sent me to the village of Dascon to report to Hakan what had happened, he stayed to help protect the village. While he was battling with a few stragglers, a couple of Larmat warriors went into town and took three females. My mother was one of those females. He went to save her and neither he nor she returned. Hakan allowed me to become a warrior for the village of Dascon. He took over training me. Me and Niro practiced many hours together."

"Hakan…"

"He treated me like I was part of his family. However, I have this damn scar to remind me of Rasmus and what his people did to my parents."

Nina came up to her knees and gently kissed all over his scarred eye.

"I am sorry you must look upon this mark. It can't be easy."

"What, not easy to look at your face!" She cupped his face in her hand. "You are the most handsome man I have ever seen. That scar takes nothing away from that, in fact it gives you a fiercer look." She playfully growled at him. Her heart leapt, hearing his rich deep laughter.

"Nina I want to ask you something?" Demos couldn't look at her.

Nina sat back down next to him. "What is it?"

Demos took several deep breaths. He didn't know how to ask her this.

"Hey, just say it." Whatever he wanted to ask must be very important to him. She could barely breathe and wished he would just come out with it.

"Nina, I want to be your mate." He turned to her and pulled her into his arms. "Will you join with me?"

"Demos…I…" Nina pushed at his chest and he let her go.

"I will provide well for you and I will protect…"

"Shh." She placed her hand on his mouth softly. "I know you would. But…"

"You don't want me as your mate." Demos started to stand up.

Nina grabbed his arm and pulled him back down. The pain in his deep voice was almost too much for her to hear. "I do want you Demos. I would love to be your mate, but…I just can't do that joining ritual thing that seems to be so important to your people."

"I don't understand."

"Robin told me what is involved with this joining ceremony. For two weeks warriors will challenge you for me. Now we both know that no one is going to do that. And while it doesn't bother me in the least, I have a feeling it will look bad for you. I don't want that."

"I don't care if not one warrior challenges me for you. It is unimportant to me."

"But it seemed like a big deal to the rest of them."

"I don't care about that part Nina. If a warrior challenges me I will fight my best to keep you. But if no one comes forward…I just don't care." Demos grabbed her hand.

"And then there is that joining feast thing. I just can't dance around and try to seduce a room full of men, well that part wouldn't be that bad, but having to pleasure all of those men in front of you, I just can't do that."

"It is our tradition Nina."

"Exactly, but I can't do it. I am going to shame you again." Nina lay down on the grass. "You are going to think this is silly."

Demos lay down beside her. "Tell me what you are thinking."

"It's just a silly little girl fantasy."

"Tell me Nina."

"When I was a little girl, I had dreams of being swept away by a knight in shining armor. He would ride up on his steed and just take me away from everything. He would take me to a beautiful land and there we would be married. And of course we would live happily ever after. That was just a silly romantic notion, but still…" Nina looked up at the beautiful sky. "My whole life I wanted someone to love me, so much so that I let a lot of men walk all over me. Now I found you and I just can't let our life together start with some big orgy." She looked over to him. "Do you understand at all?"

"I think so."

"I would say yes in a minute to joining with you Demos if we could just go away somewhere and make it official. Your people's traditions seem very important so I doubt they would allow this to happen. So I don't know what to do."

"I will give you time to adjust, maybe you will become less against the tradition of the joining feast once you get use to everything on Malka."

Nina just smiled at him. She just couldn't go through with the joining ceremony and she doubted no matter how long he gave her she would never want to do it. She knew this wasn't fair to him.

"I will wait for you Nina." Demos kissed her hand softly. "You warm my heart."

"Demos…" She felt the tears start to build. She nuzzled next to him. "I love you too." She barely got out. She held him tightly as she heard the background noise of the village. Everyone was preparing for the Festival of Life. She forced herself to think about that.

"Nina, it is okay," Demos said as he stroked her hair. His deep voice was so soothing.

"I know, just hold me for awhile."

"I will hold you as long as you want, my flower." Demos felt her melt into his embrace.

∞∞∞∞

Nina held little Zenos in her arms as Robin fussed over what to dress him in. Niro and Demos were standing off on the other side of the room talking with Tomar and his mate Sasha.

"Your child is beautiful," Safon said as she stared at him lying there in Nina's arms. If only Niro and the other males weren't in this room. Killing these two females would be easy, then she could throw Zenos off the balcony before she made her escape.

"Thank you." Robin smiled holding up a light blue infant's dressing gown.

"What should we be wearing?" Nina asked.

"Something pretty." Robin went over to her closet and pulled out a light blue dress that matched Zenos' outfit, then she pulled out a light pink gown. She walked over to Safon. "Here, I would love for you to wear this. This is a little long for me, so I am sure it will fit you fine."

"Thank you." Safon smiled, taking the dress from her.

"Little one," Niro's voice boomed, starling Safon.

"What do you think?" Robin held up the outfit she had picked for Zenos to wear.

"Perfect." Niro went over to Nina and took Zenos gently from her. "Though I can't wait for the weapon maker to make him his first sword." Niro playfully bounced his son in his arms.

"Oh, that won't be for awhile yet, Niro."

Nina smiled at the way Niro fussed over his son. She felt Demos' hand on her shoulder. "You should go get ready Nina," he said quietly.

"Allow me to help your female," Sasha said.

"Would you like that?" Demos asked Nina.

Nina looked up at the lizard woman. She was a bit uneasy about leaving with a bunch of lizard people, but she didn't want to cause any more trouble for Demos. "That would be nice, thank you." She smiled up at Sasha.

"You will be well guarded." Demos kissed her gently and watched her leave with the Rundals.

Niro summoned Rai to escort Safon back to her chamber so she could get ready. "Demos stay with Robin for a little while. I must make sure the Rundals' eggs have arrived safely.

"Yes Niro."

Niro kissed Zenos and handed him back to Robin. "Be ready by time I return, little one."

"Okay." She sat Zenos on the bed and started to change his clothes.

"Robin may I ask you something?" Demos took his guard position by the wall.

"Of course you can."

He told Robin about Nina's fantasy of being whisked away by a knight in shining armor. He was puzzled by Robin's big smile.

"Oh Demos I think every little girl on Earth has that fantasy. A steed is a horse. I guess you would say it would be like your conja." Robin placed Zenos in his basinet. "I can talk with her more about the joining ceremony, and maybe Kelila can help. But it sounds like Nina has been hurt a lot during her lifetime, which would make her tough as nails attitude make more sense."

"What am I going to do?" Demos said quietly.

"Give her time. I think once she gets use to everything she may be more open to the traditions of Malka."

"Thank you."

"Your welcome. Please keep an eye on Zenos while I get myself ready."

"Of course." Demos walked over to Zenos' basinet. Zenos was busy sucking on his toes. Demos smiled and offered his finger for Zenos to grab onto. Demos wouldn't be able to have children until he drank the sacred juice of the mandra plant. This was given at the joining ceremony. Up until now Demos didn't dare to think of fathering offspring, but now…seeing Nina holding Zenos in her arms…

"My son has a strong grip doesn't he?" Niro asked as he walked back into the room.

"Yes, he is going to be a strong warrior."

"Our sons will train together." Niro patted Demos on the back. "You better ready yourself for the ceremony, and your female looked nervous around the Rundal so you better bring her comfort."

"Yes Niro." Demos quickly left the room.

ഇ഻ഇ഻ഇ

Nina was surprised how comfortable she felt around Sasha. After she got use to Sasha's reptilian features, talking with her was quite enjoyable. She learned how the Rundal arrived on this planet and that they were the last of their race. She heard how the Dascon clan has been so generous and helpful to them.

Demos entered the room and just watched as Sasha curled up Nina's short brown hair then carefully placed little purple flowers throughout her hair. He smiled seeing Nina enjoying herself. Sasha always had a way of making anyone comfortable.

"Look at your female Demos." Sasha stepped back and presented Nina.

"You are so beautiful Nina."

Nina's breath caught just watching the way he looked at her. His words were nice to hear, but the way he was looking at her let her know he meant what he said. She felt so beautiful at this moment.

"You must hurry and get ready Demos. Would you like me to groom you as well?"

"Thank you." Demos followed Sasha into the bathing chamber. Nina followed them.

Demos removed his sword, then his loincloth and slowly stepped into the water. Sasha gathered some oils and scented soap.

"You are going to bathe him?" Nina asked, feeling a bit of jealousy creeping up.

"Of course." Sasha walked over to the bathing chamber. Demos walked over to her and stood up, dripping wet. Sasha began to soap up his body, when she was finished he submerged himself back into the water.

"Don't worry Demos' female, though I have grown to appreciate the barbarian male's form, nothing compares to a Rundal male."

"I…ummm…"

"I can see your distress. You have nothing to be jealous over. I am simply honoring Demos as the warrior he is." Sasha climbed into the bathing water and went to work shampooing Demos' long mane. Nina watched every movement of Sasha's hands. She wanted so much to be the one bathing him.

Demos submerged himself again then slowly climbed out of the water. Sasha followed then proceeded to oil down his body. Nina followed the movement of her hands taking in every glorious inch of his body. Sasha brought over a black leather loincloth and begun to dress him. She placed on his bracelets and handed him his sword. Demos then sat down on a chair so Sasha could brush out his beautiful hair.

"Allow me." Nina went over to Sasha and took the brush from her hand. She slowly brushed out his hair letting her fingers run through the silky strands.

"Braid it now," Sasha said.

Nina lovingly braided his hair and Sasha wrapped a band of leather around the bottom securing it.

"You are beautiful Demos," Nina said as he stood up and looked at her. He reached out his hand and gently stroked her cheek.

He turned to Sasha. "Thank you for honoring me."

"You have earned much more than this Demos." Sasha looked to Nina. "Demos has protected my people for years. He is Niro's best warrior."

Demos could see the pride in Nina's eyes and it made him feel like Niro's best warrior. More so than the countless battles he has been in.

"Now I must ready myself."

"Oh, do you have…" Nina didn't know how to phrase it.

"I am eagerly awaiting the birth of my hatchlings." Sasha bowed respectfully to Demos and she gave Nina a hug before she left.

"If I didn't want to mess your well-groomed self up, I would fuck the hell out of you right now," Nina said, looking Demos up and down.

She gasped when he lifted her up in his arms and carried her to the bed. He positioned her on her hands and knees and carefully lifted her dress up. He let his loincloth fall to the floor then impaled her with his hard cock. He rode her hard and fast, they didn't have much time, but he wanted her, oh damn did he need her pussy right now. He gripped her hips as he drove his cock faster and faster. He bit his lips trying to hold off from coming. When she arched up and cried out he allowed his orgasm to happen.

"Stay like this," he said. He walked over and grabbed a washcloth and then carefully cleaned her pussy off. He put back on his loincloth as she straightened herself up.

"Whoa," was all she said as he smiled and led her out of the room.

᠄᠄᠄᠄

They entered a large chamber, which to Nina looked almost like a ballroom. In the center of the chamber was a rather big fountain. It looked like it was freshly constructed just for this festival. Nina looked out over the sea of warriors, some with females most without, they were dressed similar to Demos. What few women that were here were dressed similar to her. Around the fountain were several Rundal males. She could easily tell they were males by the way they were dressed and built. Besides, she noticed the female Rundals had different shading to their bodies. The males were blacker in color, where as the females had like a greenish tint to them. Of course the males were much larger than females as well. The Rundals' form wasn't that much different than a human male or female, except of course for their reptilian features and tails. Beautiful music and a joyous atmosphere filled the room.

"Wow," she exclaimed. She noticed off to the side were tables full of all sorts of food and off to the other side were what appeared to be basinets. She also noticed Niro and Robin were seated at the back of the chamber with Tomar and Sasha seated next to them. Robin had Zenos cradled in her arms.

"Come Nina." Demos led her toward the fountain where they were seated.

"Have their babies hatched?" Nina asked, looking around.

"They have and the survivors will be brought into the chamber in a little while."

"Survivors?"

"Only about half of their young will be hatch successfully."

"Oh that's awful."

"Not for the Rundal, they celebrate the half that have been born and don't dwell on what has been lost."

Nina noticed the lights were dimming and she felt Demos grab her hand gently. She looked around and saw Sabrina and Saa, Jamie and Samson, and a few other warriors who were seated by the fountain. She looked behind them and spotted Rai and Safon standing off to the side with several other warriors. Rai didn't look too happy.

"Why are we seated so close to the fountain?"

"We are the warriors the Rundal trust most. We are being honored." He smiled down at her.

"Oh…" She watched as a couple of large Rundal males carried large silver cups filled with oil, they slowly poured the oil into the water. "Oil and water, hmmm almost like us in a way, Demos." She chuckled quietly.

"Watch, my flower…" One of the Rundal males lowered a torch into the water setting it on fire. "Maybe we are like water and oil but together we bring each other warmth and our love is beautiful to behold."

"Demos." She wrapped her arms around one of his and watched the beauty of the fire dancing on the water. She could feel the warmth of the flames. He seemed to always know the right words to say.

"Look." He pointed to the chamber side entrance.

"Oh my…" she exclaimed as she watched the Rundal hatchlings being brought into the room and gently laid down in their basinets. She watched Robin and Niro carry Zenos over to where the Rundal hatchlings were and they laid him in one of the basinets.

"Let's celebrate the beginning of new life." Tomar raised his goblet.

Nina gently took a goblet from the tray offered by a Rundal female.

"Each new life that we were blessed with signifies hope, signifies a new beginning." Tomar drank from his goblet, so Nina followed drinking the slimy liquid much to her surprise tasted pretty darn good. She felt Demos' hand on her arm making her stop drinking the delicious liquid.

"That is pipom and it only takes a little to get you drunk." He smiled down at her.

"Oh."

"Now let's feast and celebrate the birth of Niro's son and my people's hatchlings."

"Can we go look at the little Rundals?" Nina asked.

"It is required." Demos handed her a small plate of raw meat.

"What is this for?"

"You will see." Demos escorted her over to the basinets.

Nina looked into one of the basinets. "Oh how cute," she cooed. She started to place her hand into the basinet but Demos stopped her. "But…" She smiled down at the little lizard, its body form looked like a human infant, the only difference was the little tail and the texture of its skin. The face was reptilian looking but still it was so darn cute and she wanted to touch it. Again Demos stopped her from doing so.

"It will eat your fingers, Nina." Demos took a piece of meat and held it over the hatchling's mouth it quickly snapped the meat away from his hand and ate it.

"Holy shit," Nina whispered, seeing the razor sharp teeth of the hatchling.

"Only a Rundal can hold its young. The hatchling only goes by scent. Feed the hatchling, but be careful."

Nina held up a piece of meat and the hatchling snapped it up. She moved over to the next one and the next until the plate she carried was empty. She stopped by Zenos' basinet, he was cooing and seemed to enjoy the attention. She looked up and saw Niro standing close by keeping a watchful eye on his son.

"There is only one Dascon baby?" Nina asked, looking for others.

"Yes, there were two babies born in other Dascon villages but that is it. My people are in danger of dying out if more children are not born soon."

"Demos I didn't realize it was that bad."

"That is why the Rundal found Earth. As you see we are compatible with the Earth females," he said, looking down at Zenos. "What Robin has done is give my people hope. If Sabrina's child is just as healthy as Zenos, then my people will have a chance." Demos turned to her. "I am sorry you were taken from your planet Nina." He felt her hand go up to his mouth. This made him smile, this was her way of trying to comfort him, to let him know it was alright, a simple gesture, but one that carried so much meaning.

Joyous music filled the chamber. Nina allowed Demos to lead her to the tables full of food. Some of it looked really disgusting and she guessed it was probably for the Rundal, especially when Demos led her to another table. There were all sorts of wonderful looking food at this table. She decided not to ask what any of it was and simply enjoyed.

She liked talking with Sabrina, Jamie and Robin. Safon however was rather quiet. Demos was always there by her side. Occasionally she would hear him growl at another warrior that got too close to her. The only disturbance of the evening was when Niro commanded that Rai leave. Rai had consumed too much pipom and he was becoming increasingly obnoxious. Demos grabbed Nina's hand and headed over to the basinets, there he drew his sword. Rai was too close to the hatchlings and Zenos for Demos or Niro's liking. Rai decided to leave and at least pretend to follow Niro's orders willingly. But Nina could see the hate in his eyes and when she looked up at Demos, she knew he saw it too.

"Demos I don't trust Rai at all," Nina said quietly.

"Neither do I." He placed his fingers under her chin and tilted her face up so she was looking into his eyes. "You will make a fine warrior, my flower." He smiled at her.

Oh she loved his smile, never had she seen a man's smile so beautiful before. "You would know," she replied.

"Demos go play with your female. I have warriors posted just in case Rai decides to try something," Niro said.

"If you are sure you don't need my sword."

"Go on." Niro smiled down at Nina then went to Robin and his son.

"Well you heard your leader." Nina grabbed Demos' hand and led him toward the group of Rundal who were dancing a most beautiful dance. "Can we join them?"

"Yes, but…"

"Don't be a chicken."

"Chicken?"

Nina dragged Demos to the middle of the floor. She noticed some of the Dascon warriors were dancing pretty provocatively with Rundal females. "Ummm, they aren't going to, you know?" she quietly asked Demos.

"Yes, they will have sport with the Rundal females, if the female wishes them too."

Nina already knew that sport meant sex here on Malka. She couldn't begin to mentally picture what sex would look like between a human male and a Rundal female. "Have you done that before?"

"Done what?"

"You know have sport with…" She gestured toward a Rundal female.

"Yes I have. Now I thought you wanted to dance." Demos pulled her close and started moving to the sexy beat of the music.

"You had sex with a lizard woman?" she whispered.

"Yes, what does it matter?"

"Oh nothing really, but now I am curious." She looked at him move, oh damn was he turning her on.

"Dance Nina," he purred in that deep voice of his.

She moved her body next to his. "I want you Demos."

He grabbed her hand and led her out of the chamber. He headed outside. The moons were bright and cast a romantic glow over everything.

"Two moons too." She smiled looking up at them. They could still hear the music playing. "Dance for me Demos," her voice begged.

Without hesitation he began moving his body in the most seductive manner. The best male exotic dancers on Earth couldn't hold a candle to the way Demos moved. His strong body moved with such grace, such...mmmm. Nina pulled at his loincloth wanting it off him now. He helped her to remove it.

"I need to taste you," she said, coming down to her knees before him. She took his cock into her mouth and sucked feverishly. She rolled her tongue over the head of it. "You are so amazing looking Demos, you set my body on fire just looking at you." She took his cock back into her mouth.

Demos couldn't take his eyes off of her. She made him feel so male. Her hands wandered up his body enjoying the feel of him, and it showed. "Let me taste you female," he growled.

"No, oh no, I want to taste every inch, hell I want to worship this beautiful body of yours. Lay down, oh please Demos."

He did as she asked. Her hands touched every part of him. Her mouth licked and sucked every inch of him. He could feel his frenzy starting to build, but he kept it at bay. She made him feel so desired, so loved, oh so wanted. He didn't want to spoil it by not controlling his frenzy. He groaned when she removed her covering and slowly squatted down and sheathed his cock.

"Damn your cock is so huge. It fills and stretches me like no other male has ever done before." She slowly rode him, enjoying his cock sliding in and out of her.

The pleasure she wore so beautifully on her face was driving him mad. He gripped her hips and helped her ride his cock.

"Oh yes, Demos…oh yeah fill me, bury that big ass cock in me."

He lifted his hips up burying himself to the hilt in her.

"My male," she purred. "My beautiful male."

"Nina!!!" he cried as his orgasm overcame him.

"That's it my male, fill me with your cum, oh yeah."

"MY FEMALE!!!" he cried over and over as wave after wave of pleasure pulsed through him. His seed pumped from his cock; never had he came this much before. He felt her collapsed down onto him and he held her tightly against him.

"Don't move Demos. Keep your cock buried in me." She sounded so content, so satisfied he didn't dare move. He didn't think he could move right now anyway.

122

Chapter 13

"I have something for you," Demos said as he kissed her good morning.

"Really, what is it?"

"Get dressed." He looked so excited that it made her hurry up getting ready.

"Okay what is it?" She joined him out on the balcony of their chamber.

He had his hands behind his back as he stood there smiling at her.

"Stop teasing me and show me what it is."

"Here." He handed her a most beautiful sword. "I told the weapon maker to make your sword as beautiful as you are."

"Oh Demos." Her hand lovingly, but carefully, ran down the etched blade of the sword. She looked at the golden hilt and guard. Everywhere different flowers were engraved on the sword. "It is almost too beautiful to use."

"Is it too heavy?"

"No, it's perfect. Thank you Demos." She smiled up at him.

"I am happy you like it."

"Like it, hell I love it!"

"I have arranged for your training to begin this morning if you would like?"

"Sweet!" she exclaimed. "Oh but wait, I can't train in a dress."

"Robin had this made for you." Demos handed her a bundle that was wrapped up.

Nina opened it up. There was a tunic-looking shirt and a pair of Capri-looking pants, both in a navy color.

"You can only wear that when you train, okay?"

"Okay." She hurried into the chamber to change into her training clothes. "Well what do you think?" She modeled her outfit for him.

"You would look good in anything, Nina, but I prefer you in your traditional dress."

"Well I couldn't very well wear what you are wearing could I?"

"Hell no!" he quickly replied.

"Let's get to the training grounds. I am eager to get started."

"Wait." He took her sword from her and placed it in a leather sheath. "Wear it like I do." He watched her carefully pulled the strap of the sheath over her head then adjusted it so it sat comfortable on her back. She grabbed his arm and let him lead the way.

She could feel the stares from the other warriors as they passed them on their way to the training grounds. She looked up at Demos, he paid them no mind as they headed out onto the training grounds.

"What is this?!" Rai exclaimed. He was covered in sweat and had obviously been training hard already. "Demos, there is no way a female will train on these grounds."

Nina stepped back when Demos drew his sword. He said nothing but simply charged at Rai.

"Oh shit!" Nina reached back and drew her sword, too.

"Nina no!!" Demos growled.

She quickly put her sword back, then she noticed two other warriors doing the same. Did she do something wrong? She wondered as she watched Demos and Rai battle. She saw two more warriors draw their sword, and head over toward Demos.

She was about to call out to Demos, then watched in amazement as Demos beat back the other two warriors then returned to his battle with Rai.

"Stop this!!"

She turned around when she heard Niro's voice. She let out a sigh of relief when the two men immediately obeyed.

"Demos' female is wearing a sword!" Rai protested.

"I know, I gave him permission to train her."

"What?!"

Nina could see the startled looks on several of the other warriors' faces, too.

"Great Niro…a female wielding a sword this is not right," a very large warrior injected.

"Demos, why would you allow your female to be put at risk like this?" another added.

"Hey back off. This is no one's business," Nina spoke up. "Niro said it was fine so it is, so just step back."

"You allow your female to speak to warriors this way," Rai growled.

"I will not train with a female," another warrior added.

"I wouldn't allow any warrior to train with my female." Demos stood in front of Nina, daring any of them to try anything.

"Enough of this, go back to your training," Niro said. All the warriors but Rai obeyed right away.

"This is wrong Niro and you know it." Rai looked at Nina as though she was some disease. "If I would have kept you female I would have beaten you into submission."

Niro drew his sword the second Demos charged at Rai. Niro pushed Nina back as he stood in front of her.

"Stay put," was all he said to her as he kept his eyes on Demos and Rai fighting.

"Stop this please," Nina begged.

"Rai has insulted Demos one to many times. But don't worry, I will not let them kill each other."

Nina couldn't breathe as the battle seemed to go on forever before Niro stopped it. Demos would have killed Rai. "Now go Rai, next time I will not stop Demos."

Rai growled at Niro and walked away.

"Why did you stop me?!" Demos' voice boomed.

"Now wasn't the time for this Demos."

"Like hell it wasn't."

"You better control your anger."

Demos sheathed his sword. "Forgive me Niro."

"I must train, keep your female on this end of the training grounds. When the other warriors have grown use to seeing her here then she may train beside them."

"Yes Niro."

Nina watched Niro walk over to the other side of the training grounds. "Demos I am sorry."

"For what?"

"I am causing you so much trouble. Maybe training me isn't such a good idea after all."

"Don't worry about it Nina. You want this so I will make it happen."

"But…"

"Shh, enough female." Demos gestured over to a large tree.

Nina watched as a terrified weaker male approached them. His sword was a lot smaller than Demos was and she suspected Demos had this smaller sword made too.

"He will be your training partner. I am afraid I will hurt you if you spar with me. Maybe after awhile we can spar together."

"Whatever you think is best. You are the expert here. But ummm, I think maybe this guy might be too afraid of you to be able to train with me."

"Don't be afraid Laigne," Demos said.

"If I hurt your female you will kill me." Laigne's body trembled.

"Not if you haven't done it on purpose. If you don't train with her I will indeed hurt you."

"Oh geez Demos scare the crap out of him. Hey wait aren't you Robin's helper?" Nina asked.

"Yes." Laigne kept looking up at Demos.

"I said I won't hurt you, now stop trembling."

"Yes Demos."

They proceeded to train. Demos showed her the basics and she took to it like she was born to wield a sword. Demos enjoyed her enthusiasm. Even Laigne seemed to catch on quickly to what Demos wanted him to do.

Rai watched from the distance with Safon standing by his side. "This is an outrage," Rai growled.

"Maybe you should think about doing something about it."

"Shut up female. However you do have a point. I should kill Demos."

"I wasn't referring to Demos."

"What are you talking about?"

"It seems to me that you would make a better leader than Niro."

"I know I would." Rai looked down at her. "Maybe I should be leader."

She cringed seeing his arrogant smile. If somehow Rai did manage to kill Niro there would be no way Niro's loyal warriors would let him live. But this would be good for the Larmat Clan. Still she doubted very much Rai could kill Niro. Anyways, she was so close to her goal. She was getting real close with Robin, now it was just a matter of waiting for the right time. She kept the small vile of safon juice ready. She tapped her bracelet, which held the precious juice. Niro only left Demos to guard Robin alone. No other warrior was given this privilege. This buffoon Rai would come in useful to get Niro out of the room. She was so close, so freaking close to doing the task Rasmus wanted. But her time was running out, no doubt the scout Niro sent has reached the village of Tanton by now. It wouldn't take him long to realized she had lied. Two more days at most was all she had to kill Robin and Zenos. Now with this little spat between Rai and Demos, Niro was sure to want to discipline Rai himself. She had to make sure she was by Robin's side.

"I have to go back to Robin's chamber soon," she said.

"Niro will not allow it until he or Demos is there. Let the little bitch wait a few." He grabbed her and pulled her to him. "Besides, I need you to suck on my cock for awhile."

"No, let me go."

"That wasn't a request female."

"Rai let her go. I forbade any warrior to touch her. Don't tell me you have gone against this order as well."

"Niro…of course not."

"Come Safon." Niro glared at Rai. Something would have to be done about Rai. Though he hated to kill a winner of the Trials, he feared he would have no choice but to do so.

"Yes Niro." Safon followed Niro back to Robin's chamber. She watched Niro lavish attention on Robin and Zenos as her heart pounded in her chest. The time was almost here. She saw the way Niro glared at Rai. Now she would only have to wait for Demos to stand guard.

"Are you okay?" Robin said, gently taking Safon's hand.

"Rai scared me a little."

"You are safe here, don't worry." Robin led her over to the small table where some tea was laid out.

"Little one, as soon as Demos comes back from training Nina, he will stand guard over you two females and Zenos. I have something of great importance to deal with."

"You can go now if you want. I am sure we will be okay for a little while."

"No, not until Demos is here."

Safon rubbed her bracelet. Soon, so very soon, Robin and Zenos will be dead and Demos would be forced to watch as he sat there helpless to save them. But more importantly she could return to Rasmus. After she told him the good news then finally she would be his mate.

"Are you sure you are okay?" Robin squeezed her hand.

"I will be shortly." Safon smiled at her.

Chapter 14

Nina combed out her hair as she mulled over today's events. Demos was going through a lot for her and not once has she heard him complain. He would only say it was what she wanted so he would get it for her. Nina picked out a nice pale green dress. She liked the way the silky fabric of the covering, as Dascon women called the dress felt against her body. She carefully finished getting ready and made sure to put on Demos' favorite scent.

"He has gone through a lot for me and what have I done for him," Nina whispered to herself. She has been so unwilling to bend about so many things. The joining ceremony was the big one. She wanted so much to be able to let Demos keep his traditions, but...she just couldn't do the joining feast orgy thing.

Demos had told her to stay in their chamber while he went to guard Robin. Niro only trusted him to stay alone with Robin. She was going to join him but wanted to take a bath first, now she was stuck in this chamber until he returned.

Nina sat down on the large bed. The faces of the warriors on the training ground wouldn't leave her mind. Demos risked much to fulfill her wish to train with a sword and he did so freely. Guilt started to gnaw at her. Maybe she should go talk to Niro and see just how much Demos was risking training her. If the price was too high she just couldn't allow him to do it.

"Yeah, now to somehow get to Niro's chambers," she sighed. She was risking Demos getting mad at her again for walking around without an escort, but at the same time she really needed to talk with Niro. How in the heck was she going to find Niro without Demos knowing that she was disobeying him again? "Okay if Demos has to guard Robin that means Niro won't be in the chamber…" Nina said to herself as she stood up and started pacing around the chamber. "Where would Niro go? Hell it could be anywhere. Maybe he is dealing with Rai, but if I disturb him while he is doing that…argghh!" Nina thought and thought then it hit her, Niro hardly left Robin alone for more than a couple hours at a time. All she would have to do would be to wait a little while then head for Niro's chamber. If she was lucky she might be able to intercept Niro before he made it to his chamber. And the worse thing was, she should just go to Robin's chamber and take Demos' anger while she waited for Niro to return. Either way, she had to talk to Niro. If Demos training her was something that would reflect badly on him, then he would have to stop her training.

Nina went back to the bed and lay down. She would wait a little while then make her way to Robin's chamber. God she hoped she wouldn't have to deal with any horny warriors on her way there.

ೞೞೞ

Demos stood by the wall in his guard stance in Robin's chamber. He tuned out what the women were saying to give them a little privacy. He heard only bits and pieces of their conversation. Robin and Safon were talking about Safon's village. Niro went to deal with Rai, Saa and Samson went with him. Either Rai would accept his punishment or he would die by Niro's sword, either way Demos was glad that Niro was finally taking care of Rai. How Rai won the Trials amazed Demos, though he heard that Rai had cheated somehow. It didn't really matter. Rai didn't act like one of Niro's best warriors, and to Demos that is what counted most.

"May I prepare you a special tea from my village?" Safon asked Robin.

"Do we have everything here you need?"

"Let me see." Safon looked over the various roots, herbs and leaves set out. Robin's weaker male Laigne enjoyed creating new teas for Robin. So of course since Robin liked this Niro provided a large variety of roots, leaves and herbs for Laigne to use.

"Do you need my assistance?" Laigne said as he set out items needed to brew some tea.

"No, thank you." Safon looked at the weaker male. "Robin your servant looks so tired, would it be alright if I dismiss him?"

"Laigne, you do look awfully tired. Please go rest."

"Thank you Niro's mate." Laigne hurried from the room not daring to even glance at Demos.

"I wish he would just call me Robin."

"You know he can't," Demos added.

"I know, Niro would get angry." She saw Demos nod his head in agreement.

"Demos would you like to sample my special tea?" Safon asked.

"I better not."

"Oh come on Demos, she is going through all the trouble it's the least we can do. And besides you might like it."

"Alright."

"Thank you Demos." Safon smiled at him.

Safon had to really focus as she carefully empty the liquid safon from her bracelet into Demos' cup. It would only take ten minutes for it to paralyze Demos, then he wouldn't be able to move for at least a half an hour. She poured the tea making sure to set Demos' cup aside. It would do her no good to paralyze Robin.

"Here." She handed Robin a cup, then she grabbed the one for Demos and brought it over to him. "Great warrior," she said, bowing her head and handing him the cup.

"Oh this is good, Safon. You must give Laigne the recipe for it," Robin said as she sipped her tea.

"What do you think Demos?" She watched as he drank down the tea. She knew he wouldn't linger on it the way Robin was doing.

"Very good," he said.

"Oh thank you." She took the cup from him and headed back to the tea cart. "Would you like some more?"

"No thank you."

Safon kept looking over to Demos waiting for the safon root to start working. Robin was talking about something but she couldn't focus on what Robin was saying.

Demos shifted his feet. He started to feel light headed. His feet became numb. "What?" he whispered, then he drew his sword. "What have you done to me, female?!" he growled. He tried to move forward but his legs refused to work. The next thing he slid down the wall to a seated position and his sword fell from his hand.

"Demos?" Robin started to get up, but Safon pushed her into the bed.

"He will be alright, but I am afraid he won't be able to move for a little while. But he can still hear and see everything." Safon pulled out one of Niro's daggers she had taken earlier from his dressing chamber.

Robin rolled off the bed and hurried over to Zenos' basinet.

"I will make it quick Robin." Safon headed over to her.

Demos tried to move but his body was completely paralyzed. Damn it, a female was the assassin, damn it. He swore over and over in his mind. He tried so hard to will his body to move. He couldn't let Robin and Zenos get harmed. But it was useless, there was no way he could fight the effects of the drug she gave him.

"I will not let you harm my baby." Robin stood in front of the basinet ready to fight. "Why? Why would you do this?"

"For Rasmus, my leader, my mate."

"You are a Larmat, but…"

"Hair dye, you dumb female. Niro never thought to suspect that the assassin was a female. Of course he wouldn't. These dumb Dascon warriors can't allow themselves to believe that a female is capable of such things. Now I am going to kill you and Niro's son, then Rasmus will destroy this village. Finally, the Larmat will control all of Malka." Safon looked over to Demos. "Remember this great Demos, a female brought you down. I was told to let you live, but I want Rasmus to have a trophy to post at the main gates of the Larmat village."

"Leave him alone!" Robin cried out.

"Shut up, I plan on taking his head back to Rasmus and there is little you can do about it since you will be dead." Safon charged at Robin.

Demos focused and focused but nothing was going to make his body move. He would have to sit here and watch Robin and Zenos die. He watched Safon knock Robin onto the bed and Robin trying her best to hold back the dagger from piercing her flesh. He knew it wasn't her safety or her life Robin fought so hard for, no, it was Zenos she was trying to protect.

"Demos I know you are going to be mad but…" Nina froze in the doorway.

"Get in here bitch," Safon growled as she held the dagger at Robin's throat.

Nina did as she asked and closed the door behind her. "Demos." She quickly looked back over toward Robin when she heard Safon grunt. Robin had managed to slip out of Safon's grasp and now she had placed her body over Zenos' basinet, using her body as a shield for her baby.

Without thinking Nina charged at Safon before she had a chance to get close to Robin.

"What do you think you can do female?" Safon growled as she pointed the dagger at Nina.

Nina positioned herself, she had to get that dagger out of Safon's hand.

"Nina, behind you, hurry," Robin yelled.

Nina quickly looked behind her and saw Demos sitting there leaning up against the wall. She turned back to Safon then looked back quickly at Demos; she saw his sword laying there beside him. She pretended not to know what Robin was talking about. She had to get Safon to follow her. She made a couple of attempts to get closer to Safon only to have Safon lunge at her. Each time she did this she would move back a little. Until finally she was close enough. She heard a soft clanging noise and quickly looked back to see that Demos somehow had managed to push his sword closer to her. Quickly she squatted down and grabbed the sword with both hands.

"Enough playtime Earth female." Safon came at her. Nina dropped down and did a leg sweep knocking Safon down. But Safon quickly came back to her feet.

"What did you do to Demos, bitch?"

"I drugged him. He will not be aiding you I am afraid. I have no time to keep messing with you." Safon lunged at Nina again, this time slicing her arm.

Nina kicked Safon hard sending her flying. Moving faster than she thought she could Nina charged at Safon pinning her under her. She used the hilt of Demos' sword to smash Safon's hand, forcing her to release the dagger. Nina quickly knocked the dagger away.

"What are you waiting for, you have bettered me!" Safon growled.

Nina wanted to plunge the sword into Safon, but she just couldn't do it.

"What is going on here?!" Niro's voice boomed through the chamber.

"This bitch tried to kill Robin and Zenos and she hurt Demos." Nina climbed off of Safon. She gasped when Niro drew his sword and decapitated Safon right in front of her.

Niro stood above Safon's body and looked over to Nina. The horrified look on her face told him she had never witness someone being killed before. He quickly went to her and pulled her over to Demos. "Check on your protector." Niro dropped his sword and hurried over to Robin and Zenos.

"We are okay, Niro." Robin wrapped her arms around him. "If Nina hadn't come in, I…" Robin broke down in tears.

"Demos?" Nina ran her hands over his face. She could see him blinking.

"She must have used safon root," Saa said. He headed over to the tea cart. He crushed up a various mixture of herbs and roots, then he mixed it in some water. He gently pushed Nina aside and then laid Demos down. "I will pour this down your throat, try to drink it."

Nina could only watch as Saa slowly poured the liquid into Demos' mouth. He slowly came up to his feet. His head still woozy and his body moved stiffly.

"Nina…" He grabbed her and pulled her into his arms. "Are you hurt?"

"No, just a small cut. Are you okay?"

"I am now. Thank you Saa." Demos bowed his head to him. "Stay here and don't interfere, promise me."

"I promise."

Demos walked over and picked up Niro's sword. He went over to Niro and came down on one knee holding Niro's sword above his head. "I have failed you Niro. I offer my life as payment for my failure."

"What?!" Nina held her breath. No, what was she going to do?

Niro walked over to Demos and took his sword from Demos' hand. Demos lowered his arm to his side and bowed his head.

Nina wanted to yell, hell, to beg Niro to spare Demos' life, but she promised not to interfere. She might make it worse, or even blow any chance Demos had if she did interfere.

"I don't want to take your life Demos. Rise up." Niro sheathed his sword.

Demos slowly came up to his feet. "Thank you Niro. But I must pay for my failure."

"Your female saved my family Demos. Besides, I didn't see that Safon was the one we were looking for in the first place. It was all right there and I wouldn't let myself see it, because she was female." Niro bowed his head toward Nina. "I owe you, Nina."

"Then spare Demos any shame or guilt."

"Demos has saved my life and Robin's many times, nothing would make me see him as lesser."

"Niro," Demos whispered.

"What has happened here will not be repeated?" Niro ordered.

Samson and Saa nodded their heads in agreement.

"Demos go rest. The effects of the safon root will linger a bit."

Nina followed Saa as he helped Demos back to their chambers. She waited for him to leave then she crawled onto the bed with Demos and snuggled up to him.

"Nina, you fought well," he said as he pulled her closer.

"I am glad I decided to risk your anger, oh boy am I glad. Are you going to be okay?"

"I will be. But I will never allow myself to be in that position again."

"Shhh, you rest." Nina held him tight. The events of the afternoon started to sink in and it almost made her want to throw up. She could have lost him. Robin and Zenos might have been killed. She took a deep breath and let it out slowly.

"I know Nina, I feel the same way," Demos said as he nuzzled his chin to the top of her head.

Chapter 15

Niro had sent one of his scouts carrying the banner of the messenger. Both clans honored this banner. The messenger's only task was to deliver Safon's head to Rasmus. To ensure the messenger's safety he was to only place the wooden box at the gate of the main Larmat village.

Demos had Nina stay with Robin while he and several other of Niro's finest warriors discussed matters. Niro's actions, though warranted, would no doubt cause the Larmat to attack.

"What's going to happen?" Nina asked. She noticed that Robin hadn't let Zenos out of her arms the whole time she sat with her.

"Niro wouldn't say, though I feel there will be another attack on one of Dascon's villages. Niro sent several warriors to Tanton. Since Safon claimed to be from this village Rasmus will no doubt try to destroy this small border village. This was all Niro has told me so far."

"Is Demos going to this village?"

"I don't know Nina. But if it does look like Rasmus will attack this village, Demos will probably lead his warriors to assist."

"Why send Demos?"

"Niro will go too, Nina. He will have to defend his people, and where Niro goes to battle Demos is always by his side."

Nina felt her stomach knot up. Rationally she knew Demos was a warrior, so of course he would go to battle if needed, but her heart didn't want to think about this. "How much time before they go?"

"It will take Rasmus time to organize his warriors. And of course Niro would have to know for certain where Rasmus was going to attack. It will be a few weeks at least before they go."

"Nina."

Nina quickly came to her feet when she heard Demos' deep voice. She went over to him and wrapped her arms around him tightly.

"You may go be with your female Demos. It will be a couple of days before we know what will happen," Niro said as he went over and sat down next to Robin. He gently rubbed Zenos' head and wrapped his arm around Robin.

Demos grabbed Nina's hand and led her back to their chamber.

"Are you going to have to go to battle, tell me the truth?"

"Yes, Nina." He saw the stricken look on her face as she slowly sat down on the bed. "I am a skilled warrior. You needn't worry about my safety."

"Well, I am afraid I will be worried about you. You could get killed. Especially since that Rasmus has it in for you. Damn it Demos why do you have to go?"

"To protect my people."

"Rasmus wants you dead."

"Rasmus wants all Dascon warriors dead."

"Well, he wants especially you dead. Please Demos…" She reached up and grabbed his hand. She brought it to her face and gently nuzzled against it. "Don't go Demos."

"My flower." Demos came down to his knees in front of her. He grabbed her hands and squeezed tightly. "I have to go if Niro calls for warriors. I am one of the most skilled warriors of Dascon, my sword will be needed. If I don't go many younger warriors may die. It's not arrogance Nina, it is fact. I must go and lead my warriors." He reached up and cupped her face in his hand. "Niro will go, so I must. Please understand Nina."

"I do understand. But I don't like it." Nina couldn't stop her tears. "When I saw you just sitting there not moving after Safon drugged you…it scared me. If you go to fight Rasmus…" She reached out and pulled him into her arms. "I am so afraid you will die. I can't lose you."

"You won't lose me." He gently stroked her back as he held her.

"You can't guarantee it. Demos I love you damn it, please don't leave me now."

"Oh, my little flower. I will come back. Please understand I swore an oath to use my sword to protect my people. Why do you think I have been training so hard? If my people are in need, Nina I have no choice but to aid them."

"I know Demos."

"I love you, my little flower and nothing will stop me from coming back to you. The love you give me will make my sword more deadly and accurate. If I fought so hard before, now I have even a greater reason to fight well." He looked deeply into her eyes. "I have you to come back to."

He slowly kissed at her falling tears. She pulled him down into the bed with her. She wanted his body as close to hers as possible. Finally she found the man of her dreams, she couldn't lose him. She didn't care anymore that this was a rather strange planet, didn't care that she would never see her home again. Demos had become her home. She would live anywhere as long as he was with her. Never had she felt so loved and cherished before. She had became so use to men treating her badly that she had given up hope of ever finding her knight in shining armor. Hell, she given up hope that a good man even existed. Who would have ever thought that she would find him here. Yes, Demos was pushy and a bit uncivilized. He even got on her last nerve. But it didn't matter. She felt loved for the first time in her life. She didn't need to hear his words of love, she could see his love in his eyes, in his actions.

"Shhh, Nina please stop crying."

She could see the pained look in his eyes. Her pain tore at him and she could actually see how much.

She reached up and pulled him closer wanting to taste his lips. "I want to feel you deep inside me," she whispered against his lips. She felt him remove his covering and pull her dress up. The head of his cock was now poised at the opening of her pussy. He looked deeply into her eyes as he slowly slid his cock into her.

"I want so much to be your mate," he whispered as he slowly thrust. "I will find a way to make you completely mine."

"I am your female, Demos. You warm my heart." She saw his eyes lit up as she tried to phrase her love for him the way a Dascon female would.

He laid more of his body weight on her as he continued to slowly thrust. He wanted to feel her body moving under him. He reached his hands under her and squeezed her ass. "Nina," he whispered into her ear as he thrust faster.

She loved his deep voice, mmm, even more so when he was making love to her. She wrapped her legs around his waist. His body weight felt good on her though she labored to breathe. He must have sensed it because he removed his hands from her ass and propped his upper body up.

"Demos," she purred as she grinded her pussy against him. She closed her eyes and enjoyed the feeling of his cock going in and out at a steady rhythm. "All of it, oh bury your cock in me." She tightened her legs around his waist pulling him closer. "Yesss," she hissed when she heard him groan with pleasure. "I want to hear your pleasure Demos, growl at me. Oh yes," she moaned. His deep growls excited her.

"Take your pleasure, female," he groaned.

"More Demos, I want more." She moved her head side to side as he rode her faster and faster. "Yes, more, more, harder, harder, harder!!!"

"Come now!" he growled loudly. He watched every moment of her orgasm. Nothing in this world was more beautiful than the look of pleasure on her face. He felt his own orgasm build. "Look at me." She slowly opened her eyes and stared into his eyes.

"I am going to come again," she moaned, but still she gazed deeply into his eyes.

"Yess!!!" he yelled out. "See the pleasure you bring me female." He pulled his cock out of her quickly and let his cum splash onto her body. "You do this to me."

"Demos." She rubbed his cum over her body. She reached down and grabbed his cock. "Let me clean you."

He quickly straddled her. She grabbed his ass and pulled him up to her head. She licked at his cock tasting her own sweetness on it.

Demos grabbed the headboard of the bed to steady himself. His cock already getting hard again as she continued to lick every inch of it. He moaned loudly when she began to suck on him, taking him deeply into her mouth. His hips began to thrust following the movements of her mouth sliding up and down his shaft. He felt her hands knead his ass as she swallowed his cock.

"I am going to come," he groaned. She smacked his ass then pushed up on his hips removing her mouth.

"Watch," she said as she stroked his cock.

146

He looked down just as his cum shot into her mouth. She continued to stroke until every drop of his cum was out. She gave the head of his cock one last lick. She chuckled seeing him crashed down on the bed beside her. That exquisite look of satisfaction on his face pleased her.

"Oh the things you do to my cock, female," he said breathily

"Mmm, my pleasure, I adore your cock." She snuggled up next to him.

"I need to sleep now. You have worn me out." He chuckled.

"Well, let's sleep, as long as I wake up just like this."

"You will." He kissed the top of her head and pulled her closer.

❧❧❧

"Rasmus." The tower guard hurried into the room carrying a box.

"What is it?" Rasmus removed the woman who was kneeling down before him sucking his cock. Rasmus didn't like that look on the guard's face. He quickly put back on his covering as the guard set the box down on the table. "What is in the box?"

"I…just look great Rasmus."

Rasmus walked over then slowly lifted the lid of the wooden box. The strong odor of decaying flesh assaulted his nostrils. Rasmus took a second to adjust to the awful smell. He peered into the box then fell to his knees.

"Rasmus." The woman who had just been servicing him ran over. The guard however slowly backed up to the door wanting nothing more than to leave the room.

"ARRRGGH!!!" Rasmus yelled as he drew his sword and ran it through the woman's chest. He slowly came to his feet. "NIRO!!!" he yelled. He turned toward the guard. "Bring me five Dascon females now," he growled.

"Yes Rasmus." The guard hurried out of the room. Within moments he came back with five dark haired females.

"Damn you Niro, damn you," Rasmus thundered.

The guard stood there in shock as Rasmus proceeded to decapitate all five females. Females were so rare and still they are killed. What a waste. If it wasn't for his fear of Rasmus the guard would have stopped this. "Send Niro these Dascon sluts' heads and tell him I will destroy a Dascon village."

"Yes Rasmus."

Rasmus grabbed the box that held Safon's head and took it into his private chambers. "Safon," he whispered as he put the lid back onto the box. He should have never sent her to do the task. Why didn't he send some other female? He knew why, Safon was the only female who would have had a chance of completing the task. Niro's family still lived. Safon's sacrifice was for nothing. Rasmus stayed in his chamber until nightfall, mourning the loss of his beloved Safon. When he emerged he announced to his warriors that they would attack Tanton as soon as possible.

"Leave no one alive. Kill all of them."

"Even the females and offspring?" one of the warriors asked.

"Yes, but we will stake the females and offspring up, line the town with their corpses. Let Niro see what my vengeance can do. When he arrives there will be nothing but ashes and death. But we will wait for him. Once he has taken in the destruction of one of his beloved villages, then we will attack."

"But Rasmus…"

"Speak."

"Niro is powerful, you saw him take on several of our warriors when he rescued his mate. And Demos will surely be with him."

"Are you a coward, Tarrant?"

"No, Rasmus."

"Let Niro come, I welcome it. As far as Demos is concern, I will kill him myself. Now we must plan our attack."

Chapter 16

Nina was growing impatient waiting for Demos to come back. He had gone to see Niro early in the morning and now it was almost noon. She had to fight the urge to find him. After everything that just happened she didn't have the heart to disobey Demos' request that she stay in the chamber until he returned. She had no doubt that Niro and Demos were going over some sort of battle plan.

Nina had dressed in a very beautiful, light blue gown that seemed to shimmer with every movement. She indulged Demos' request that she have flowers placed in her hair. She welcomed the company of Jamie as she helped her to get ready. Jamie's joining feast was tomorrow, which brought up feelings of guilt in Nina.

She walked over to the balcony and gazed out across the village. Everything seemed so peaceful and quiet. The air was clear and the colors of the huts and landscape seemed to pop out. She could catch a glimpse of the two large jeweled towers. Robin had told her that Niro's father Hakan had the towers built for Niro's mother, Kelila such a grand romantic gesture, Nina thought.

She was startled when she heard the door burst open. She was expecting to see Demos and was surprised to see Niro entering the chamber.

"Follow me."

She thought it was odd that Niro stood there with a strange grin on his face. Her curiosity made her follow him. He led her out onto the training grounds. Robin, Sabrina and Saa were also on the training grounds. They too had smiles on their faces.

"Stay here," Niro said. He then went over to Robin.

"What is going on?" Nina asked. She heard a flapping noise and quickly her eyes turned toward the sky. There flying toward her was Demos on the back of his conja. He was wearing ceremonial battle dress: black leather loincloth, a golden circlet on his head, his sword was sheathed in a golden scabbard. Never had she seen a more glorious sight. She backed up a little as the conja landed a few feet from her. She couldn't speak or take her eyes off of him.

Demos dismounted and headed over to her where he came down on one knee before her. "I am your knight in shining armor, Nina, and I have come to take you away and make you my mate." He stood and scooped her up into his arms. He carried her over to his conja. "Do you want me as a mate?" he asked.

"Yes," she quietly replied.

He helped her up onto the conja then climbed on behind her. He held her tightly to them as they took flight. They soared high into the air.

Nina enjoyed the sensation of flight. She knew Demos wouldn't let her fall. "Where are we going?"

"You will see, my flower."

Nina looked behind them and saw two conjas flying not too far behind. "Someone is following us."

"I know, it is Niro, Saa and their mates." Demos landed the conja in a small wooded area just beyond the village. Nina was surprised to see Tomar, Sasha and a few Rundal warriors waiting by a flowered arch.

"What is going on?" Nina asked as Demos helped her off the conja.

"We are going to be joined."

"But I thought…what about the joining feast?"

"We are being joined partly as Rundal and partly as my people." Demos led her over to Tomar.

"Demos will say the words of his people, Nina. If you agree take his sword."

Nina nodded her head and watched Demos come down to his knees unsheathing his sword. "I offer you my protection; my sword is a token of that." He raised his sword and offered it to Nina.

Nina gently took the sword from his hand. "Kiss the hilt if you agree, Nina, then hand it back to Demos." Nina kissed the hilt and handed it back to Demos without hesitation.

Demos gracefully sheathed his sword and bowed his head. "I offer you my body to use for your pleasure. I offer you my heart, so you can bask in the warmth that fills it. I offer my life to you to do as you will. My sword that you have accepted will protect you from any danger. My mate, I give to you my soul and everything that is mine." Demos took the bracelet off his left wrist and held it firmly in his hands. "In your eyes I have proven I am the strongest warrior, that I have the ability to protect you and our future offspring. Do I also have your heart, body, and soul?"

"Demos, I give you my heart, body, and soul and give myself over to your protection." Nina extended her right arm and looked to Robin to make sure she had done this right. She smiled seeing Robin nodding her head in approval.

Demos rose to his feet and placed the bracelet on her wrist, giving it a squeeze to mold it to her wrist. Then he turned to Tomar. Nina did the same.

Tomar had a golden goblet in his hand. "For all here let it be known that Demos and Nina are now and forever joined. Demos, by drinking this sacred juice, your seed will produce offspring. May your young be strong and wise." Demos took the goblet from him and drank down the liquid.

Demos took Nina's hand and looked deeply into her eyes. "As it is the custom of the Rundal. Nina you must proclaim Demos your mate before everyone here," Tomar said

"Demos is and will always be my mate."

"By saying this in the eyes of the Rundal you two are joined. By Demos saying the sacred words of his people, in the eyes of the barbarian race you are joined. Congratulations."

"Congratulations," Robin and Sabrina squealed as they hugged her tightly.

Nina saw Niro and Saa patting Demos on the back. Tomar passed around glasses of wine.

"As it is custom on Earth, we will toast the bride and groom." Tomar lifted his glass. "May your life together be long and happy."

Nina was so happy, she couldn't remember ever being this happy before. Demos must have planned all of this. He remembered her girlish fantasy, that was the sweetest thing. He even made sure to include something from her home planet. She felt her tears fall.

"What is wrong?" Demos hurried to her.

"Nothing, I am just so happy at this moment."

He took Nina into his arms and looked over to Niro with a confused look on his face.

"Earth women sometimes cry when they are happy," Niro said. Malka women rarely did this, their tears were usually in sadness.

Demos scooped up Nina and carried her over to his conja. He climbed on still holding her in his arms. She turned around and wrapped her arms and legs around him. She needed to be close to him.

"You are going to make it hard for me to concentrate female." He chuckled as they took to the air.

Nina needed him now. She reached down and grabbed his cock. He quickly undid one side of his loincloth. She moved the fabric aside then lifted her dress, being careful not to fall off the conja. She felt Demos' strong arm hold her tightly making sure she wasn't going to fall. She lifted up a little and sheathed his cock. Slowly she rode him as his strong arm held her tightly, his other arm he wrapped around the reins holding them steady on the back of the conja.

"More, female, take more of my cock inside you," he groaned.

Nina tightened her legs pulling him closer. "Yessss," she hissed as she took his cock to the hilt in her. She felt the conja head toward the ground and she tightened her grip on Demos. She opened her eyes and saw they had landed. As soon as the conja stopped Demos jumped down.

She noticed they were back on the training fields. "Demos…" she softly protested.

"I need to ride you, female," he growled. He came down onto his knees still holding her tightly to him. Then he flipped her over until she was positioned on her hands and knees. She knew what he wanted and it made her body quiver with anticipation.

"Oh Demos," she moaned as he filled her again. He slammed his cock into her, harder and harder as he growled. She felt his body lean over hers. Her breathing became rapid as she eagerly waited for him to pin her under him. She moaned loudly when she felt him bite down on her shoulder growling like an animal as he rode her faster and harder.

"No other male will touch you," he growled, riding her faster and faster. "Take your pleasure female, let me hear it. Scream out so all males will know how much pleasure my cock brings you."

"Yes Demos, yes!!!" she yelled. "I love your cock, fuck me harder. YESS!!!"

Demos arched up and drove his cock deeper and harder into her. His orgasm was slow to build, it was so exquisite and seemed to last forever as he continued to drive his cock into her. He could hear himself screaming out her name as the pleasure intensified until his seed spurted into her. Over and over, stream after stream he came until finally he collapsed down onto her.

"Holy hell, Demos," Nina exclaimed. "All your moaning and growling made me come twice. What the heck was in the juice Tomar gave you?"

"It is from the mandra plant. Niro said it would make my pleasure last longer," Demos said, trying to catch his breath.

"He wasn't kidding on that. Oh this is going to be so much fun," she playfully chuckled.

"He said it will also make my cum taste sweeter."

"Really? It tasted pretty damn yummy before." Nina smiled then kissed down his chest. She took his now hard again cock into her mouth.

"Oh no you don't, I want to taste you too." He grabbed her and positioned her so her pussy was in easy reach of his tongue.

Nina moaned when she felt his greedy tongue lap at her. Damn did this man know how to eat pussy, more importantly he enjoyed every second of it. She leaned over and took his cock into her mouth. She sucked fast and feverishly, eager to taste his cum. She felt his hips rise up as the first stream of cum filled her mouth. It was sweet and tasted like candy, she greedily drank down all he had to offer. She sat up feeling his tongue go deep inside her. "Demos, oh yeah..." she purred. She squatted over his face and heard and felt him moan. His tongue licked everywhere, she was almost dizzy with pleasure as he brought her to multiple orgasms. She felt his hands grip her hips and his tongue began to explore her ass. The unexpected pleasure of it made her have another orgasm. "Demos I don't think I can take much more," she said as her body quivered.

"I am not done yet, female." He buried his face in her pussy, moving her hips back and forth. He licked and sucked as she rode his face. She felt his nose and chin rub everywhere driving her mad with pleasure. When her last orgasm hit he sat her firmly down on his face and held her there until he had lapped up all her sweetness. She climbed slowly off his face then laid down on the grass.

"I am exhausted, damn do you know how to eat pussy, baby," she sighed.

"You taste delicious, my flower." He laid his head on her stomach.

"Speaking of delicious, your cum taste like delicious candy now. Why is that?"

"Something in the mandra juice."

"We better get dressed. Warriors will be coming out to train soon." Demos jumped to his feet and fastened back up his covering. Nina quickly put her dress back on. Then she followed Demos as he put Bella back into her pen.

"Now come my mate, let's go back to our chamber," he said, lifting her up and carrying her back into the leader hut. Nina just contently laid her head against his chest.

Chapter 17

Nina enjoyed her daily training with Demos and Laigne. Hell, even Laigne seemed more relaxed around Demos now. Maybe now that Nina was officially Demos' mate made the tension ease.

Niro was upset by the box he received with the women's heads in it. He had been assembling his warriors to head out to Tanton. Nina knew Demos would be leaving in just a couple of days. She didn't let herself think about it, instead she threw herself into training and enjoyed every moment she had with him.

Nina had finished a series of guarding techniques when she spotted Rai on the training field. "I thought that Niro…well either imprisoned or killed Rai," Nina said.

"Rai was imprisoned but with the upcoming battle, Niro gave him a chance to redeem himself," Demos replied.

"Oh, hell no, I don't want that asshole fighting next to you. He is liable to kill you."

"Don't worry Nina, Rai is staying here."

"I am not sure I like that either."

"Rai must prove himself to Niro or he will be executed when Niro returns. So I wouldn't worry about him causing any trouble. Samson will be in charge and I am sure he will station Rai far away from you. Matter of a fact I insisted he did just that. Now you and Laigne run through the sequence again while I practice with Saa."

"Okay, ready Laigne?"

"Yes." Laigne came at her with all he had and she successfully blocked each one of his attacks. They ran through the sequence several times, then Nina practiced some of her attack moves.

"Permission to speak," Laigne said as they sat down to rest for a moment.

"Sure, talk whenever you want."

"I can't until you speak to me first. But anyways, I wanted to say that I will watch over you while Demos is gone. I will not let Rai hurt you or Robin for that matter."

Nina looked over at Laigne. She liked this new confidence he had developed over this last week. He wasn't nearly as strong as any of these warriors, but he sure was quick. "Thank you Laigne." She smiled at him.

"Nina."

She watched Laigne quickly come to his feet and step away from her when Demos approached.

"What is it?"

"Ready your sword." He drew his sword and waited for her. "I will show you what it feels like to have a male of my strength hit your sword."

Nina got ready to block his attacks. She braced herself when he swung his sword down at her. Her whole sword vibrated from the impact. She lifted her sword again blocking the next and the next until finally he knocked her sword from her hand.

"You can't fight a warrior like me head on. You want to evade and wait for your moment. Let's try again." He watched her, even though she was exhausted she picked her sword back up. He swung his sword again, this time she moved out of the way. "Good Nina, remember your training you received on Earth, use both your sword and your fighting skills together." He saw the focus in her eyes. He charged at her again, this time she evaded then

159

kicked him back. "Very good, but still keep your distance. Here, put this on your sword."

Nina put the leather sheath on her sword. "Why am I doing this?"

"You are going to try and kill me. This way you won't really cut me and I won't cut you."

Demos charged again. He was just too good and he ended up mock killing her several times, but Nina didn't want to give up. The focus and determination in her brought great pride to Demos. He charged again. She evaded him several times, landing a few kicks in. She watched and waited, when she thought she found an opening, he managed to block her. His skill was most impressive. She managed to knock him down with a sweeping low kick, but he instantly got back up to his feet. She was pleased that he didn't just allow her to win. If she did manage to win, it would be a well earned victory. She saw his arms go up for one of his strong slices. She moved quickly and managed to stab him in the gut. He lowered his arms and smiled at her.

"Very good, my flower, very, very good, you used your smaller size to your advantage."

She smiled back, she could see the pleased look on his face. Even though every muscle in her body ached it was worth it to see that look in his eyes.

"Demos, Niro wants you in the battle chamber," a warrior said.

"I will be right there." Demos stroked Nina's cheek. "You have done very well today. Why don't you soak in a nice warm bath now?"

"Too bad you can't join me," she whispered.

"I will as soon as I speak to Niro." He gave her ass a playful swat then headed over to the leader hut.

Nina noticed that ever since they were joined, Demos allowed her more freedom to walk around. She also noticed that once a warrior spotted Demos' bracelet on her wrist, they didn't bother her. Nina was enjoying her new freedom, though Demos still wouldn't allow her to venture beyond the village without him.

Nina soaked in the large bathtub. The warm water felt so good on her aching muscles. She loved the fact Demos trained her so hard. He treated her like any other warrior, which meant a lot to her.

"Nina."

She quickly opened her eyes hearing Robin's voice. "Robin, what's wrong?"

"You will want to get dressed."

Nina climbed out of the bathtub and Robin helped her to get dressed. "What's going on?" Nina asked as she quickly brushed her hair out.

"The warriors are getting ready to go to Tanton. Rasmus' warriors are only a few days from the village, so they have to go now."

Nina could see the worried look in Robin's eyes, hell she felt the same way. Her heart pounded in her chest as Robin led her out to the conja stables. She spotted Demos, he was in full battle gear. He wore bits of armor, one piece covering the shoulder of his sword arm, pieces on his knee and a piece that covered where his heart was, other than that he only wore his loin cloth, sword and a dagger strapped to his thigh. She wanted him covered from head to toe with armor. She ran to him and threw herself in his arms. She held him tightly. This very well could be the last time she ever held him.

"I love you so much, Demos," she said, holding him tighter.

"I love you more than anything, my flower." Demos lifted her up and kissed her deeply. "I will come back to you, Nina."

"You better. Please be careful."

Nina could hear Robin and Sabrina crying in the background. She quickly looked around and noticed the few Malka women, who were seeing their mates off, weren't crying at all, but instead were smiling.

"Why are they smiling?" Nina wrapped her arms around Demos.

"They want their mates to remember their smile."

Nina looked over at Robin and watched her wipe her tears and then she too smiled. She saw Saa telling Sabrina something and then Sabrina smiled as well.

"I want to cry Demos, but your custom is much better I think." Nina smiled warmly seeing that it meant so much to Demos.

He kissed her one last time then mounted his conja. Nina went over and petted the conja gently. "Bring him home Bella."

"She will."

Nina went over to him and nuzzled her cheek against his hand. "You warm my heart, Demos."

"My flower, you are my heart." He bent down and kissed her.

Nina heard the sound of a bellowing horn and Niro giving the order for them to leave.

"Come back to me, my warrior."

"I will, I swear it." Demos looked at her one more time then took flight following Niro.

Nina heard all the women start to cry now. She went over to Robin. "They will be back."

"Females, please go back to your chambers," Samson said. "Your males must not hear the sound of your tears."

Nina watched the Malka females hurry back inside, then she felt Robin grab her hand. "Let's keep each other company for awhile," Robin said.

"Okay." Nina went back to Robin's chamber with her. Shortly after that Samson brought Sabrina and Jamie to the chamber, too.

"Niro's mate, I must go post the remaining warriors around the village. Is there anything you need or require?"

"No, thank you, please go do what you have to. Your mate can stay with me."

"This is shit." Sabrina got up and headed for the tea cart. "I don't want Saa to go fight. Isn't there warriors in that village already?"

"Niro will not allow any of his people to suffer. Rasmus will no doubt send many warriors and what warriors there are in Tanton will not be able to protect the village. Forgive me for speaking up." Laigne quickly went back to making the women's tea.

"You are right Laigne. Niro loves his people," Robin replied.

"How long will they be gone? How many warriors will return?" Nina asked Laigne.

"They should return in a few days. Battles are not long and drawn out as you said they are on Earth. I don't know how many warriors will return. But not all of them will."

"I am so scared for Niro. You know Rasmus will want him dead."

"Niro is the leader of the Dascon clan so yes, he will be a main target. But don't worry he is a very skilled warrior. Besides Rasmus would want..." Laigne stopped abruptly when he looked at Nina.

"He would want Demos dead, won't he? I mean he would want some sort of revenge or something."

"Yes, I am sorry. The scar Demos has will only remind Rasmus of his failure."

"Nina..." Robin reached over and grabbed her hand.

"Demos is the best warrior, second only to Niro, you shouldn't worry Nina." Laigne handed her some tea.

"I don't know if I can just sit here and wait, but I have no real choice do I?" Nina choked back her tears.

"We all have to wait. Jamie, I am glad that Samson was chosen to protect this village. He will do a good job, I am sure of that," Robin said.

ഇഇഇ

Nina was surprised when Kelila took her to meet Hakan. Why in the world would he want to meet her in the first place?

Nina slowly walked into the large chamber and there lying in the bed was an older version of Niro, though he didn't have Niro's green eyes. Hakan looked very ill and it made Nina a little uncomfortable at first.

"Come closer, mate of Demos," Hakan said weakly.

"It's an honor to meet you," Nina said as she went over to the side of the bed and bowed her head.

"You are a very beautiful female." Hakan got up to a seated position. Kelila placed pillows behind his back and leaned him back.

"Thank you."

"Please sit down."

Nina sat down on the chair Kelila brought over.

"Niro tells me that Demos has been training you to be a warrior." Hakan chuckled a little. "Demos tells me you are a rather skilled warrior."

"Thank you."

"Though I don't really approve of a female training, it seemed to mean a lot to Demos, so I said nothing, besides Niro had already given him permission to do so. Kelila please bring me my grandson." He smiled warmly at his mate.

"Zenos is a very cute and strong baby."

"Of course he is. Niro is a strong warrior."

"Why did you want to meet me?"

"You are Demos' mate. I wanted to go to his joining ceremony, but as you see that wasn't possible." Hakan looked over Nina. "Demos is like a son to me. I am sure he has told you what happen to his parents."

"Yes he did."

"His father Ranor was a dear friend of mine. I remember trying to talk Ranor into moving to the village of Dascon, but he wouldn't. His mate Jeneva wanted to remain in Tanton where she was born."

"Demos is from Tanton?"

"Yes, that is where he got that scar of his too. I am sure he has told you all about that too."

"But I thought the village was destroyed."

"It was, but the survivors rebuilt. Don't worry about Demos, he will kill Rasmus this time. Demos was such a young warrior when he came to me. Never had I seen such skill in a warrior that young. Demos looks like a carbon copy of his father, hell he even acts like his father use too. I am so glad that Demos has a mate. I can see the warmth you have for him in your eyes and it does this old male's heart good." Hakan just smiled and seemed lost in thought for a moment. "You know I remember training Niro and Demos together. Demos was far more skilled than Niro at first and it use to frustrate Niro so much. But not once did Demos ever rub it in or act superior to Niro, but instead he would help Niro. Demos was always so quiet and he tend to shy away from the females. Most warriors would at least look at what few females there were. They wanted to catch the female's eye. But not Demos, I think he felt that scar on his face somehow made him less attractive to the females. Kelila told me once, she noticed several females trying to catch a glimpse of Demos and of course they would watch him train, when their protectors had to bring them out to the training grounds." Hakan took the cup of tea Nina offered him. "I will miss talking with Demos when death comes for me."

"Does he talk to you often?"

"Oh yes, he has come and sat with me often. Only Niro sees me more. I am glad Demos will be here to help Niro adjust to being leader."

"It looks like you have done a fine job teaching Niro to be leader."

"My son was meant to be ruler, it is in his blood. I have only simply guided him a little." Hakan seemed to beam as Kelila brought in Zenos. She carefully placed the infant in his arms.

"I will leave you alone to enjoy your grandson. Thank you for talking to me."

"It has been my pleasure. You take care of Demos."

"I will." Nina gestured for Kelila to stay where she was. She headed back to her chambers. She welcomed the distractions Hakan gave her, but now her fear for Demos gnawed at her. How was she ever going to get through this next couple of days? She fell onto the bed and snuggled with Demos' pillow. The tears streamed from her eyes as she prayed for his safe return.

൲൲൲

"Get the females and offspring into the center hut," Niro ordered. "These are your families, you will stand guard and make sure no Larmat scum gets near them," Niro said to the warriors who lived in the village. "Demos, take your warriors and head to the south part of the village, Saa, you and your warriors to the east, Alistair, you and your warriors to the west and I will take the north. Try not to let any get past you." Niro knew how Rasmus thought, he would most certainly circle the village. They would be ready for him.

Demos headed over to the south part of the village. That feeling he had grown accustomed to filled the air, tension, hatred and fear. He tried to clear his mind as he grip his sword tighter, but thoughts of Nina kept coming to him. Her smile, the way her skin felt, her sweet voice... Demos shook his head and tried to clear those thoughts. Now wasn't the time he had to focus on the upcoming battle.

"They approach," one of the warriors said.

Demos could see the Larmat warriors charging at them. He raised his sword and let out his fiercest battle cry then headed for his enemy. The sounds of swords clashing, flesh being sliced and pierced, and the cry of the wounded filled the air. Demos sliced through the Larmat warriors that approached them. His style was to kill them quickly. It was this same style that earned him the respect of his fellow warriors and fear from his enemies.

"Push on!" Rasmus yelled.

Demos growled and headed straight for Rasmus. He could hear that Niro was right to position warriors all around the village. Rasmus did indeed circle the village. He quickly killed the warriors that got in his way of getting to Rasmus. He had faith in the warriors that fought by his side, he knew they would fight well.

"Demos," Rasmus growled. "I will finish what I started all those years ago. But first I will blind that other eye." Rasmus charged at Demos.

Rasmus was far more skilled now, but so too was Demos. Their swords clashed, their bodies doing the dance of battle. All around them warriors from both sides fell. Demos heard Niro's battle cry and knew soon he would come to the aid of his warriors. So he focused completely on his battle with Rasmus. He dodged and lunged, evaded and attacked. He couldn't find an opening to kill Rasmus. He grimaced when Rasmus' blade cut his arm.

"This time I will kill you Demos." Rasmus continued his assault. Rasmus fought with great hatred, the likes Demos never felt before.

"You will not run away this time Rasmus," Demos growled as he used all his strength with the next few hits from his sword.

"I was only a new warrior, Demos, this time you will fall and I will place your head at the gates of my village."

Demos grimaced as Rasmus' blade sliced his leg. He ignored the pain. He had to fight with everything he had; he had to force himself to focus.

"I will come back, Nina." His promise to her pushed him on. He couldn't be defeated.

An eerie quiet filled the air. The battle was won or lost, Demos couldn't tell until he heard Niro cry out in victory. Still he had to focus on this fight.

All the remaining Dascon warriors watched Demos battle with Rasmus. They wouldn't interfere unless Demos fell.

There, the opening Demos was looking for. Rasmus was slow with his right swing. He dodged and blocked Rasmus' attack waiting for that one moment. Demos yelled as he jabbed his sword in Rasmus' side. Rasmus fell to the ground laughing.

"You are mad," Demos said as he pulled his sword from Rasmus' body, at the same time he kicked Rasmus' sword away.

"You think you have won." Rasmus laughed. "You may have defeated me, but by the time you make it back to your mate, she will be dead, along with Niro and Saa's mate. And your son, Niro, will be fed to the conjas alive."

"You lie," Demos growled.

"The spy you sought Niro was a weaker male. He has no doubt convinced Rai to kill your females."

"You are a liar. Your female Safon was your spy," Niro hissed.

"She was the assassin. The weaker male, Talbot, was the spy, hell he has been a spy for the Larmat for years."

Demos looked to Niro. "Leave him here. Let the village leader decide what to do with him. Gather the dead and wounded, we leave now."

Demos placed a wounded warrior on the back of his conja and climbed in front, making sure the warrior was secure. He quickly took off following Niro. Judging by how fast Niro made his conja fly, what Rasmus said must be true.

ഇന്ദ്രഇ

Something was wrong Nina could feel it. She grabbed her sword and headed toward Robin's chamber. Robin had wanted to see her sword anyways. When she entered the chamber Robin was putting Zenos down for his nap. Sabrina and Jamie were also in the chamber. Nina was relieved to see them, at least they all were in the same place.

"Oh wow!" Robin exclaimed as she looked at Nina's sword. "Demos had this made for you?"

"Yes, he also has been training me to use it."

"Lucky you," Sabrina added. "There is no way Saa would let me train with him."

"Neither would Niro," Robin said

"Or Samson," Jamie added.

"You know you still have to teach us karate. I am sure our males won't mind if we do that," Robin said.

"Sure, after everything settles down. It will be my honor to teach you guys."

"Well I will have to wait until this little girl is born." Sabrina chuckled.

The women talked all afternoon trying to distract each other from thinking about their men. But each woman was very worried, each wondered if her man survived the battle.

"Let's get something to eat I am starved," Robin said. She rang for Laigne and asked him to bring his special dish. Robin didn't really know what was in it and she would like to keep it that way.

A disturbance was happening right outside the chamber door. The women could hear the sound of swords clashing.

"What the hell is going on?" Sabrina asked.

"I think it would be better if everyone just head for the other side of the chamber. Robin is there another way out?" Nina asked.

"No, that is the only door."

Nina hurried over to the balcony. There was no way Sabrina could climb out of here in her condition, not to mention Robin wouldn't be able to hold Zenos and climb too.

Robin hurried over and grabbed Zenos then the women backed up to the other side of the chamber. "What about Laigne? He will be heading this way any moment," Robin said as she held Zenos close to her.

"Don't worry about him, he will see that something is up. Maybe he will go get Samson."

"Yes, Laigne would do that."

Nina could see the hope coming back into Robin's face.

"I say we all grab something and beat the heck out of whoever comes through that door," Sabrina said.

"Not in your condition." Nina unsheathed her sword and stood in front of the women.

"Nina you are going to get killed if that is a big warrior out there," Jamie said.

The women were startled when someone started pounding on the door. "Oh shit, the guard wouldn't be trying to bash the door down. Don't tell me some Larmat warriors got into the city." Robin held Zenos closer.

Finally the door burst opened. "Rai!" Robin exclaimed.

"Shut up, you stupid little bitch."

Nina saw the blood dripping from Rai's sword. "You bastard…you fucking traitor."

"Samson will kill you for this!" Jamie cried.

"He has to get here first and he is no match for me. Now which one of you little bitches wants to die first?"

"You can't do this. Your fellow warriors are out there fighting to keep your people safe. Niro gave you a chance to prove yourself," Robin said.

"Fuck Niro!" Rai came at the women.

"Leave them alone!" Nina swung her sword, but Rai easily blocked it.

"Oh please, I am a grand warrior, you are nothing but a female who likes playing as if she is a male. I wonder if Demos wants a male for a mate. Yeah, I think that's it." Rai chuckled.

"Well you are going to have to come through me to get to them."

"This should be most amusing." Rai readied himself. "If any you other females try and escape while I am amusing myself with this little bitch, don't think about it, you won't make it to the door."

Nina charged at him remembering what Demos taught her. There was no way she was going to match his strength, so she would have to wait for the right moment to attack.

"When I have defeated this bitch, mmm, I am going to fuck all of you before I kill you."

"What do we do Robin? We have to help her," Sabrina asked.

"I don't know."

Nina dodged and blocked his blows, but the power of his strikes was wearing on her. She kicked him knocking him back to give herself a brief break.

"I remember your punches and kicks. I should have just beaten you up, but no, Niro wouldn't have liked that would he? That was the only reason I didn't just do it. Though I am a bit sorry I didn't force you. Some warrior saw you sucking Demos' cock, he said you looked more skilled at it than those bitch weaker males are."

"Shut up asshole." Nina charged at him again. She would have to hurry up and make her move. She was tiring.

"Enough of this, it's time to die you little bitch."

Rai lifted his arms above his head to deliver the killing blow. Nina moved quickly remembering how she got Demos in training. Her sword ran through his side. She wasn't prepared for the squishing noise or the blood that sprayed from him.

Rai fell to his knees. "You…there is…no way…you could…defeat…me." His words were labored.

Robin handed Zenos to Sabrina. She hurried over and grabbed Rai's sword. It was very heavy. She held the hilt with two hands and lifted his sword up and drove it into him. "You won't get the chance to hurt my son or Niro again."

"Robin." Nina grabbed her hand and pulled her away from Rai. Within seconds he fell to the ground dead. Nina collapsed to her knees.

"Are you alright?" Jamie said, hurrying over to her.

"Yeah, I am just tired."

The sound of many warriors approaching the chamber got their attention. "Samson!" Jamie hurried over to him.

"What has happened?"

The warriors fanned out and searched the rest of the chamber. Samson walked over to Rai's body. "Who did this?"

"Nina did, but she had to. She saved us," Jamie said.

Samson saw Nina's sword sticking out of Rai's body. He went over and pulled the sword out and handed it to her. "A warrior never leaves her sword in her enemy."

"I…"

"Demos will be proud. Here." He handed her a piece of cloth.

"I can't."

Samson wiped the blood from her sword. "The first kill is always the hardest." Samson went to the other women to make sure they were okay.

Nina felt each warrior pat her on the back. A gesture she has seen many warriors do to Demos before.

"I will post several warriors outside this chamber." Samson kissed Jamie then headed back out. Two warriors carried Rai's body out.

"Oh, Nina…they see you as a warrior. And…thank you. If it wasn't for your bravery, me and my baby would have been killed," Sabrina said.

"Yes thank you Nina," Jamie and Robin said.

"I didn't know if I could do it. I just knew I had to somehow. But that awful noise when my sword went into him."

"It's okay." Robin hugged her.

"Robin, why did you impale him with his own sword he was dying anyways?" Sabrina asked.

"I wanted him to hurry up and die. I don't know what came over me."

"Are you all alright?" Laigne hurried into the room. He had splatters of blood on his shirt.

"Yes, but what happened to you?" Nina asked.

"I was hurrying to go find Samson, or any warrior for that matter, and a weaker male named Talbot tried to stop me. So I used the dagger Demos gave me and killed him. I know it's against the law to…"

"Hey, you did what you had to, Niro will not punish you for it," Robin said.

"Thank you Laigne for going for help." Robin hugged him.

"Can I see the dagger Demos gave you? I didn't know he did that," Nina said.

"He gave this to me just a couple days ago. He wanted to thank me for helping you train."

Nina looked over the finely crafted dagger. "Very nice." She smiled.

Zenos started to cry loudly. "I better go feed him. Thank goodness he had no idea what was going on." Robin carried Zenos over to a smaller chamber.

"I would like to go back to my chamber. I am really tired," Nina said.

"I will escort you," Laigne offered.

Nina smiled and let him lead the way. Once she was in her room she collapsed onto the bed. She killed somebody and though it was in self-defense, it still weighed heavy on her. She closed her eyes and thought of Demos then drifted off to sleep.

Chapter 18

Demos landed Bella and helped the wounded warrior down. Kelila was already there to greet them and aid the wounded.

"Demos." A young warrior headed over to him. "Your female…"

"Where is she?"

"She is in your chamber." He grabbed Demos' arm as he started to head toward the leader hut. "She defeated Rai."

"What?" Demos looked down at the warrior.

"Rai tried to attack the females in Niro's mate's chamber and your female challenged him and defeated him."

"It is true Demos," Samson said as he greeted him.

"Demos!!!"

Demos looked over toward the leader hut and saw Nina running out toward him. She was okay, he had never been so relieved in all his life. He opened his arms and she leapt into them.

"Oh thank God you are alright," she said as she kissed all over his face.

"My flower." Demos hugged her tightly.

"You are wounded." She pushed against his chest and he let her down. She saw the deep cut on his arm and leg.

"Demos you must mend yourself," Niro said. He had his arm wrapped around Robin and his son cradled in the other. "Nina…I am in your debt."

"As am I," Saa said.

"I did what I had to." Nina grabbed Demos' arm. "Now let's get you fixed up. Where do we go?"

"Take him to the healing chamber. Demos knows the way," Kelila said as she cupped Niro's face in her hand. "I am so glad you are home safe, my son. Please go see your father and let him see that you are alright."

"Yes mother." Niro led Robin into the leader hut.

Nina let Demos show her the way to the healing chamber. Weaker males, a couple of females and several Rundal females were treating the wounded warriors. Nina stood by the exam table Demos was sitting on as a Rundal female tended to his wounds. Nina looked around, some of the warriors were wounded badly, and some were being wrapped up like mummies.

"Why are they being wrapped up like that?"

"It is a special healing wrap for the warriors who are severely injured. It is a Rundal treatment," the Rundal female replied.

Nina looked over to another side of the room and saw about ten warriors laid out on cots with their swords laid on them. Two of them had females sitting on the floor next to them weeping.

"Are they…dead?"

"Yes I am afraid they are," Demos replied.

"That could have been you," Nina whispered.

"But it wasn't." Demos stroked her hair.

Nina waited for the Rundal female to finish up mending Demos' wounds, then she went to him and pulled him in her arms. "I am so glad you are back. I was so worried I might not have seen you again."

"Shh, I promised I would return."

"I am beyond happy you kept that promise."

৪৩৪৩৪৩

Demos' wounds were pretty bad so Nina couldn't make love to him for a couple of days. The fallen warriors were buried in private ceremonies. Demos attended every one of these ceremonies. He explained to Nina that the warriors were cremated, and he didn't understand why Earth people buried their dead. Family or the mates of the fallen would scatter the ashes to the wind freeing the warrior's soul. The warrior's sword was given to the family or his mate.

What Nina found interesting were that all people on Malka believed in a higher being, and a heaven, though they simply called it paradise. Warriors who died in battle would go to paradise. She didn't ask about weaker males, but Demos told her all females would go to paradise. Except the ones who harmed their offspring. It was simplistic, yet beautiful the way these people thought of religion. One higher being worshipped by all, Dascon, Larmat it didn't matter they all believe in the same deity, even more incredible that this deity was seen as a female the mother of all life. The Mother was all this deity was named.

Nina spent the next few days training with Laigne while Demos watched. None of the other warriors seemed to mind her presence anymore on the training grounds. Some even allowed her to watch them train and they offered her advice. Even Laigne was allowed to do the same.

She enjoyed spending time with the Rundal females. She learned all about the Rundal culture. These reptilian beings seemed even more evolved than the people on Earth. Their knowledge of medicine was amazing. And what they could accomplish, like the spacecraft using only the primitive power sources on this planet. All of it was incredible. But more so was the way they relate to the more primitive barbarians. Not once did Nina see a Rundal treat them as if they were inferior to them in any way. The way the two races of beings helped each other was inspiring to say the least.

She especially liked spending time with Robin, Jamie and Sabrina. They all understood each other. They would talk about Earth, then compare the Malka ways to Earth. Nina was really starting to enjoy her new home.

She noticed that the people of Malka didn't waste time. Ceremonies were short and sweet. Well, except for the joining ritual, but this was only for the couple to make sure they were making the right choice. The death rituals seem short. Battles were short though sometimes numerous. In a way Nina liked this idea of making everything simple.

Demos shared everything with her. He told her what happened in the battle meetings as they were called. He knew she found all of this interesting so he told her everything. It meant a lot to her that he trusted her enough to tell her all of this. Niro was sending Alistair and a group of warriors to the Larmat main village. With Rasmus dead, now was the time to make peace. Alistair would be the acting leader for the Larmat. Niro wanted peace, but he was willing to send every warrior he had to take over the Larmat village by force. The countless, atrocious acts the Larmat people committed against one another would stop now. Females were so few in numbers that no more should be harmed. Alistair was part Larmat and part Dascon, this proved to Niro it was possible to mix the races of barbarians. Though few knew Alistair's heritage, he never hid the fact he was part Larmat, but he didn't go around announcing it to everyone either. Alistair was one of Niro's best warriors and his Larmat blood made him the best choice to govern the Larmat people. Niro knew however there would be small pockets of resistance, there always was. But if he could join the two main villages, far less Malka people would have to die in needless battles.

Nina loved the look on Demos' face when he told her what Niro was planning on doing. He had such respect for Niro. She had no doubt he would probably follow Niro anywhere.

Every so often though, she would think about Earth when she was alone. She wondered if anyone missed her, or even wondered what happened to her. Her sensei probably was the only person on Earth that cared about her.

Demos walked into their chamber and saw Nina staring out across the village. The look of sadness on her face bothered him. "What is wrong, my flower?" he said, wrapping his arms around her.

"I was just thinking about Earth." She nuzzled back against him.

"Do you miss your home?"

"Home, Demos my home is where you are. But if you mean do I miss Earth…well not really. I was just wondering if anyone missed me. It's kind of depressing knowing that no one probably is missing me."

"You needn't be depressed. There are so many here that would miss you. And you are here now, so what does it matter what is happening on Earth."

She turned around and looked up into his eyes. "You're right, it doesn't matter."

Demos smiled seeing the sadness leave her eyes. His cock grew hard when he saw the lustful way she looked up at him. She grabbed his hand and led him over to the bed.

"Take off your covering and sit down," she purred.

He immediately did as she asked. He watched as she slowly let her dress slide down her body. She gently pushed him causing him to fall onto the bed, then she climbed on top of him. He groaned when her pussy sheathed his cock.

"Sorry about no foreplay, but I needed your cock deep inside me." She rode his cock slowly feeling every inch of him slide in and out. "Lay back and enjoy." She smiled at him as she rode him a little faster.

Demos reached his hands up and cupped her breasts, kneading and squeezing. His hips started to rise off the bed as he thrusts, driving himself deeper into her.

"Oh, I am going to come already," she moaned. He quickly moved one of his hands down and slowly stroked her clit as she rode him. "Oh yes, like that baby, just like that," she purred. Demos watched the pleasure on her face as she came.

"You are so beautiful," he whispered.

"Mmmm, now it's your turn," she said, looking down at him. She grabbed his arms and pinned them above his head. He offered no resistance. She moved her hips faster, squeezed her pussy tighter. "Come baby, mmm come."

"Nina!!!" He arched up as he orgasmed. He rolled over and pinned her under him as he thrusts harder a few more times as his juice filled her.

"Oh damn I needed that." She chuckled.

"Me too." He smiled down at her.

"Come here." She reached up and pulled him closer. "Kiss me." She lost herself in his kiss.

Chapter 19

The next morning both of them were summoned to Niro's chamber, Nina didn't like the look on Robin's face. Something was really wrong.

"What's going on?" Demos said to Robin.

"Hakan is getting ready to go on the great journey." Robin turned to Nina. "He is dying."

"Oh no…" Nina grabbed Demos' hand.

"Niro is with him now, but he requested to see you Demos. Kelila will come and get you when it's time." Robin started to cry. Nina hurried over to her and hugged her.

"Demos, please follow me. Nina you may want to come with us too." Kelila's voice seemed so lifeless and she looked liked she had been crying for days.

Nina followed Demos into Hakan's chamber. Niro was kneeling on one side of the bed.

"Demos come here." Hakan's voice was weak.

"Great one." Demos knelt down on the floor at the other side of the bed.

"Don't be sad, we all knew this time was coming." Hakan reached out and grabbed Demos' hand. "Demos, your father was a good warrior, and he was and even better friend. What happened to him and your mother shouldn't have happened. I should have sent more warriors to help."

"You done all that you could have."

"No, I should have done more. Hmmm, you remind me so much of your father. It has been my honor to have trained you."

"It has been my honor to have had the chance to train with you."

"Demos, you have been like a son to me. Why do you think I would allow you to train with Niro." Hakan turned to Niro. "You remember how angry you use to get at me when I wouldn't let you train with the other warriors."

"Yes, I remember."

"Demos, seeing how you acted so much like your father I knew I could trust you. I watched both of you become the best warriors in the Dascon village and no father could be prouder."

Nina saw Kelila start to cry again. At first Nina didn't know what to do. Should she just stay where she was? She could feel great sadness coming from Kelila, she hurried over to her and grabbed her hand. Nina wanted to be of some use, at least she could try to bring comfort to someone. Kelila squeezed Nina's hand.

"Niro, you teach my grandson to be a better leader than you. The way you are becoming a better leader than I was."

"You were a grand leader, father."

"I could have been a better leader, but seeing you developing into a better one eases my conscience. Demos, I want you to help Niro just like you did when you two were fledgling warriors."

"I will."

Hakan gripped each man's hand tighter then released them. "I will miss both of you." He smiled at them. Demos and Niro rose up. "Kelila come here my female."

Demos went over to Nina and grabbed her hand. Niro left then stood off to the side. He seemed relieved to see Robin enter the chamber and head over to him. He wrapped his arms around her, almost as if he wanted to borrow some of her strength. Niro showed no emotion, none of the warriors who were in the room did. Only Niro's eyes gave away the sadness he felt in his heart.

Kelila climbed onto the bed with Hakan and lay in his arms. "I will miss you the most." He kissed the top of her head. "I am sorry I must take the journey without you, but I will be waiting in paradise for you. You have been a constant joy in my life. Even in the darkest of times, the warmth of your heart showed me the way. Thank you for everything, thank you for giving me Niro, thank you for being such a good mother to him and most of all, thank you for allowing me to be your mate."

"It was my honor to have a warrior such as you be my mate. You warm my heart so much it touched my soul." Kelila started to cry as she held him tightly. Hakan stroked her hair gently. "Niro, I am entrusting you with the care of your mother. Don't let any harm come to her."

"I will take care of her, father. She won't be lonely."

"My female don't cry, let me see your smile." Kelila looked up into his face and smiled brightly. "That's better." He slowly lowered his lips to hers and kissed her gently, then he fell back onto the bed.

"Hakan…" Kelila gently stroked his face. "Journey well, my mate." The tears fell from her eyes as she stroked his cheek.

Niro raised his hand and several somber sounding horns bellowed.

Nina felt Demos squeeze her hand tightly. She looked up into his face. She saw the tears in his eyes, but she knew he wouldn't let not one fall. She looked over to the door when she heard it open. Tomar and Sasha entered the room along with several other Rundal.

"Mother, please come with me," Niro said.

"In a moment." Kelila stared into Hakan's face then kissed him one more time. Niro reached over and helped her from the bed and took her into his arms as she started to cry profusely.

"Will you allow us to prepare him for the great journey?" Tomar asked Niro.

"Yes, please." Niro led Kelila and Robin out of the room.

"Should we leave?" Nina whispered to Demos.

"No, I will help Tomar prepare Hakan."

"Do you want me to stay?"

"Yes."

Nina watched as Demos helped dressed Hakan in his battle armor. Saa and Samson entered the room carrying a golden altar and they gently set it down by the bed. Demos and Tomar lifted Hakan's body and placed it onto the altar. Niro entered the room carrying Hakan's sword. He lovingly placed the sword in his father's hand.

"Nina you must go put on something white. I will come get you when it is time," Demos said.

"Okay." Nina went back to her chambers and put on a white dress. She could feel the sadness all around. Every so often the somber horns would bellow. She came to her feet when Demos entered the room.

"Remain silent through the ceremony." He grabbed her hand and led her to the gates of the leader hut. All the women and children wore white while the men wore their battle armor. Demos and Niro helped Saa and Samson carry the altar through the streets of Dascon village. Villagers threw white flowers as they passed then they too joined the procession. They carried Hakan to a stone altar on top of a hill that was just beyond the village. Carefully they set the golden altar down on top of the stone one.

"This shouldn't be a sad day for Hakan was a great leader for the Dascon clan. He will be missed. However now he is taking the great journey to paradise. Let's praise his name," Niro said as he lit a torch and took Hakan's sword and gave it to his mother.

Nina couldn't understand the chants the Dascon people were saying so she remained quiet. She watched Tomar poured some liquid onto Hakan's body. The people chanted louder as Niro lit the liquid on fire. The heat of the flames was so intense Nina had to back up a little. Much to her surprise the flames died within ten minutes and there was nothing left of Hakan but ashes. Each person went up and grabbed handfuls of ash and scattered it to the wind. Nina did the same, then she stood by Demos and watched as each villager scattered the ashes.

When all the ashes had been scattered everyone slowly walked back to the village. Silence filled the air, Nina knew it was to show respect for Hakan. When they made it back to their chamber Nina sat down on the bed. She looked up at Demos as he slowly came down to his knees and laid his head in her lap. Her heart broke when she felt his tears fall. She gently stroked his hair as her own tears ran down her face. She felt his arms wrap around her as he nuzzled in her lap. She didn't say a word, she simply caressed him and let him silently cry.

ജ്ഞ്ജ്ഞ്ജ

Nina headed out to the training field and was shocked to find Niro and Demos sparring. It has been a week since Hakan died and a somberness still could be felt in the air.

"Niro has sparred with everyone here this morning," Robin said.

Nina watched the intensity of the battle between the two. Niro needed this and Demos knew it, so he held nothing back.

"Niro is in so much pain. Kelila wouldn't come out of her chamber. Niro told everyone to leave her alone for awhile. How is Demos?"

"He is hurting too."

"The one thing I have learned about the Dascon people is that they heal fast, both physically and mentally. Niro will be okay. I just wished I could do more to help him."

"Why are you here at the training grounds? If you don't mind me asking."

"Niro wanted me to be here. He hasn't let me out of his sight since Hakan died."

"Demos, is pretty much the same way." Nina looked up when she heard Demos groan. Niro had him pinned under him with his sword to his neck. She went to reach for her sword but Robin stopped her.

"Niro won't hurt him."

Nina breathed a sigh of relief when Niro climbed off Demos and helped him up. The other warriors left the field. She saw Niro smile and shake Demos' hand.

"He smiled," Robin said.

Nina watched the two men talk. Whatever they were saying to each other seemed to be helping each other. "I wonder what they are talking about?" Nina asked.

"I bet they are reminiscing about when they first trained together."

"Yeah, I bet you are right. Should we leave them alone?"

"Niro, I have to check on Zenos. I will take Nina with me."

Nina saw Demos nod his head at her letting her know it was alright to go. She followed Robin into her chamber. Zenos wasn't in his basinet. Kelila was holding him as she sat out by the balcony.

"It is a beautiful day today," Kelila said as she rocked Zenos gently.

"Yes it is." Robin motioned for Nina to join her by Kelila.

"How is Niro?"

"I think he is healing. He is training with Demos."

"Like old times." Kelila chuckled. "I miss Hakan so much."

"I know."

"But I can't hide from everyone forever. My son needs me to be strong, not to mention my little grandson here."

The women talked all afternoon. They listened to Kelila relive memories, it seemed to make her feel better talking about Hakan. Nina didn't want to imagine the pain Kelila must be feeling. Hell she couldn't imagine life without Demos and they have only been together for a short time. Kelila and Hakan were together for almost fifty years.

Niro and Demos entered the chamber and Niro hurried over to Kelila. "Are you alright?"

"I will never be the same without your father, but I will be alright."

"Come Nina."

"It was nice talking with you Nina," Kelila said.

"It was my pleasure." Nina followed Demos back to their chamber. They lay in the bed together and just held each other as they drifted off to sleep.

ະະະະ

The next morning Demos took Nina to a large hut. It looked to be recently built. "What is this?" she asked as she looked around the hut.

"Our new home."

"What?"

"Niro built this hut for Robin, but when Hakan got sick they decided to live in the leader hut. Niro gave me this hut yesterday. He has decided to continue living in the leader hut."

"Oh, that was nice of him. What about Robin, I mean if he built it for her…"

"It was her idea."

"This is ours!" Nina went from room to room. "We can have so much privacy. But this hut is kind of big just for the two of us."

"Well…" Demos pulled her into his arms. "I was hoping we would fill it with offspring soon."

"Then we might want to get started on that." She slowly came down to her knees. She almost chuckled when he removed his covering really fast. "Like your cock sucked, huh?"

"Mmmm." He grabbed her head and pulled her to his cock.

Nina took his cock into her mouth and leisurely sucked on it. She loved the way it felt going in and out of her mouth, not to mention the delicious way his cock tasted. Her pussy grew wetter listening to his deep growls and moans.

"I need to bury my cock in your pussy," he groaned.

She lay back and spread her legs wide letting her fingers open up her pussy for him.

"Oh…female." He quickly positioned himself between her legs then rammed his cock into her. The force of his thrusts made her move forward until her head bumped the wall. He got up on his knees, lifted her up and continued to thrust. She wrapped her arms and legs around him.

"Deeper, mmmm, deeper," she moaned.

Demos stood up and leaned her up against a wall as he thrust harder and harder. "You want more?" he growled.

"Oh yes, tear my little pussy up."

"Yessss!" He thrust hard and fast then pulled his cock out.

"Hey…I need more baby."

Demos lowered her to the ground then positioned her on all fours.

"Yeah, baby, yeah." She knew what he was going to do.

He rammed his cock into her then bent over and bit her shoulder, pinning her under him.

"Yes, yes, oh fuck yess, take me, ride me harder," she cried out.

He thrust faster and faster, biting and growling. He reached back under her with his hand and grabbed her breast roughly.

"Yeah, yeah, oh yeah!!" She arched her back into him as she came. She cried out his name as orgasm after delicious orgasm rocked her.

"Mmmm, my female," he purred into her ear.

"Demos stand up and feed me, please."

Demos quickly stood up and stroked his cock. She got up on her knees and tilted her head back opening her mouth. His cum shot out covering her face, neck and breasts; she eagerly drank down what fell into her mouth. She reached up and grabbed his cock. She licked and sucked at the head wanting more of his sweet, sweet nectar.

"Nina, mmmm…" he purred.

"Okay, that's one room we fucked in. Let's see there are about nine more to go," she said rubbing his cum into her skin. "And we got all night in which to do it."

"Oh yeah," he sighed as he came down to his knees and took her into his arm.

"I love you Demos, you know that don't you?"

"Yes, because I can feel your love. And you warm my heart, you did from the first moment I saw you come off the Rundal ship."

Nina snuggled back into his embrace. "So would you like a son or daughter first?"

"A daughter then a son, then maybe another daughter then…"

"Whoa…let's start with the daughter."

"What room do you want to break in now?" Demos kissed the top of her head.

"Well, I want to stay just like this for a moment, then we will just move room to room."

Demos held her tightly and breathed in her scent. Nina was going to become the first female warrior. He wanted to tell her this after they looked at the hut. But he will wait. He was so proud of her and was most honored to be her mate. He knew not all the male warriors would accept this, but he would be there fighting beside her. He wouldn't worry about it now. All he wanted to do was hold her and make love to her until they both were to exhausted too move.

The End

Epilogue:

Alistair landed his conja over the hill and the Larmat main village was now in sight. He looked back at the fifty warriors that joined him on this journey. He took in every one of them. These were his warriors. These warriors had trained with him, many had fought beside him, each one he trusted.

"We will go in there peacefully, but if need be we will take the village by force." He let out a fierce battle cry getting his warriors ready for anything. He climbed down off his conja and proceeded to the village on foot. His warriors quickly follow him. All of them had their swords drawn. Rasmus was no fool and had managed to kill off any Larmat warrior that might have had challenged him to become leader. Alistair expected no resistance. The Larmat people would want some sort of order. Alistair was hoping since Rasmus was a cruel leader that the Larmat people would easily accept him as their leader.

Alistair felt pride and honor that Niro chose him for this most important task. Niro accepted him even though his father was a Larmat warrior. Alistair's mother and him were banished by her village when they found out that she had loved a Larmat warrior. He never knew his father, but from what his mother had told him, his father was a good man. Hakan allowed Alistair and his mother to live in the main Dascon village and from there Alistair quickly climbed the warrior ranks. Niro had appointed him grand warrior even though some of the other warriors didn't like it. Alistair would die protecting Dascon, he would die in service to Niro. Now it was his chance to prove to Niro that the chance he took on him was worth it. He would help bring unity to the Larmat and the Dascon clans.

In truth Alistair expected Niro to grant Demos this honor. When Alistair asked Niro why he didn't send Demos, Niro simply said that Alistair was more suited to be a leader.

Alistair was happy for Demos that he finally found a mate. He knew someday he would find a female who didn't care that he was a mixed breed. He had little time to think about such things.

Alistair and his warriors arrived at the gates of the Larmat village. A young warrior came out to greet them.

"I proclaim myself leader of the Larmat clan!" Alistair bellowed.

The young warrior pulled out his sword and simply handed it to Alistair. "This is the sword of Malin, which was taken by Rasmus, and now I give it to you freely."

Alistair was relieved that there would be no bloodshed. He entered the village and looked out across the weary faces of the Larmat people. "I will bring peace to these lands. Niro, the great leader of the Dascon clan, wishes for there to be peace."

Alistair told one of the warriors to fly back to Niro and tell him what has happened. Now Alistair would have to start the daunting task of bringing this clan back together then joining them with the Dascon clan. Niro told him once this was done, there would be only one clan, the clan of Malka. Those words touched Alistair profoundly.

Protector of My Heart

Robin Stevens never thought that her ordinary life would change in an instant. But when a large barbarian warrior from the planet Malka burst through her bedroom and carries her off to his world, her whole life changes forever.

Niro, the son of the Dascon clan leader Hakan, falls instantly in love with the little female that he was sent to collect. The females on his home planet are few in numbers due to a strange illness that wiped out half of them, still more were lost to the battles that continue to rage between the Dascon and Larmat clans. Though the earth women look as though they might be able to become mates for the strongest of Barbarian warriors, Hakan orders that only two would be taken, to make sure they could adjust to Malka.

Niro claims the right to be Robin's protector. Robin has no idea that by doing this Niro has proclaimed his love for her and his intentions of wanting to be her mate. The strong-willed Robin must learn to fit into the seemingly male dominated society of Malka. But together Robin and Niro find a love that will joined them forever.

Available now

"Who's Your Daddy?"

There is nothing quite as sexy as an alpha male. Come on, you know it's true. This anthology contains twenty-two of the hottest short stories paying homage to this sexy breed of man. Whether you want to be the alpha male or be loved by him there is a story in here for you. Warriors, Lovers, Husbands, Businessmen, Masters, oh the list goes on.

An ensemble of talented writers of erotica will tantalize you with their sizzling tales of the alpha male. Enjoy!

Contributors: summersub, Thea Hutcheson, Michelle Houston, Inga Mahn, D. L. King, Dani Benjamin, John Irvin Long, Ann Cory, Robert Buckley, Cynthia Richards, Geneva King, Teresa Noelle Roberts, Andrea Dean Van Scoyoc, Mark James, Raven Young, Terry MacCoy, Bes R. Walker, Gwen Masters, Oya, Jennifer Metz, Brian Rosenberger, Justus Roux

Available now!

For a teaser of each story go to www.justusroux.com

Justus Roux's Demon Hunter Series:

Keeper of My Soul
Heavenly Surrender
The novella Forever which is in the anthology Breathless
Ayden's Awakening

Not even Hell could keep him from her

Keeper of My Soul

Miranda Williams lived a normal life until a tall, blonde, handsome stranger named Michael Varzor appeared in her life. He wasn't your ordinary run of the mill stud muffin, but one that could leap four stories into the air, run at mind numbing speeds, and oh yeah, who hunted demons for a living.

Miranda is quickly pulled into Michael's world when he has to protect her from a demon named Syn. Miranda can't believe that this sub world exists. Michael has to be crazy or even more terrifying that his tales of Heaven, Hell and Purgatory are true. Endanger of losing her mind and her heart Miranda must believe in her instincts and trust Michael.

Michael Varzor was a paid killer in his mortal life but after his death, he was pulled from the grayness of Purgatory by a man named Asurul. Michael was trained to become a demon hunter so he can protect Asurul's son Ayden. Suited for a life of a hunter Michael had learned long ago to numb his feelings. He swore to never love another woman again, never to give a woman that kind of power over him. But one look at Miranda sends him into a spiral. Wrestling with his pass and trying to fight the present Michael now has to battle with a demon that is stronger and more cunning than any before. Michael must allow Miranda into his heart or both of them will lose their souls.

Available now

Heavenly Surrender

Gabriele Conner is the only female demon hunter. Though Asurul was reluctant to train her and only did by request of Isa. Gabriele has proven herself a valuable asset to Asurul. With her skill and dedication, he knows his son Ayden is well protected with her guarding him.

Gabriele doesn't quite know what to make of their new guest Ryker Brower, a Special Forces soldier that she and her fellow hunters Ryo and Saban rescued from certain death at the hands of Kali, a powerful Demon General. Ryker's training and skill may prove useful in baiting the demon to them. The more time Gabriele spends with Ryker the more she is drawn to him. Her feelings for him trigger painful memories of her mortal life. On top of this Kali has taken the Archangel Kannon as her lover, making her even more deadly. Gabriele must pull herself together and focus on her enemy, protecting Ayden comes before all. However, when Ryker is taken by Kannon she can think of nothing else than saving the one man that is the other half of her soul.

Available now

A collection of Justus Roux's short stories that will leave you….

Breathless

Plus the two novellas:

"Forever"- Ryo had lived a lonely existence when he was mortal. Even now as one of Asurul's Demon hunters he keeps his past pretty much to himself. While Ryo mended the wounds from an earlier run in with a demon, Isa showed him an image of Jasmine, his soul mate. Jasmine is running for her life and he comforts her in her dreams while he mends.   Ayden, the man Ryo must protect has awoken, but he is weak. The powerful Demon General Manus is close by. The fates have finally granted Ryo love, but will he be willing to risk everything to keep this love
 "Forever" is another exciting edition to Justus Roux's Demon hunter series

"Master Drake"- Drake comes back to his island after his stay with Xanthos. He misses his three pets Rapture, Wrath, and Lust. But Drake is the Master of this island and must hide his pain. Only Jessica, his beloved wife can help him adjust. Drake must train two new pets that Michael has brought him to replace Rapture and Wrath. Plus he has agreed to help train Jade, Master Nikolai's submissive. "Master Drake" is a tantalizing continuation of Justus Roux's Master Series.
Available now

Ayden's Awakening

Ayden came to Emily in her dreams. Was she the one he had been searching centuries for? Could she finally bring him salvation after endless years of pain?

Ayden was cursed from the moment he was born. He had to find his soul mate or suffer the pain of love lost over and over. Now after centuries of searching he believes he has finally found the one woman that could free his tormented soul. However his fear of destroying her keeps him from finding her. Until he has no choice but to find her in order to save her. A multitude of demons have been unleashed on Earth, and their target was Emily.

Ayden and his demon hunters face the battle of their lives. Now that Ayden's true purpose is revealed the leaders of Heaven and Hell will stop at nothing to destroy him and his hunters.

"Ayden's Awakening" is the exciting conclusion to Justus Roux's Demon Hunter series.

Available now

Printed in the United Kingdom
by Lightning Source UK Ltd.
108616UKS00001B/13